Keith Allan

5 STORIES

Combo

Table of Content

About The Author

Writing has been a collection of experiences gathered from a variety of careers. After finishing at UCSD, I spent years as a keyboard/composer, completing an album and working with a few established musicians. In my thirties, I went back to school and earned a teacher's credential and later a M.A. Through many years as a teacher, I worked as a teacher instructor and developed a number of curriculums in mathematics. After retiring, I worked as a photographer, and at one point acquired over a million Instagram followers. In the past year, I have focused on writing short stories. My inspiration has come from my past careers as well as many years of watching movies of all types. I enjoy my readers, and hope my writings come as an inspiration to those that find a rich enlightment in the world.

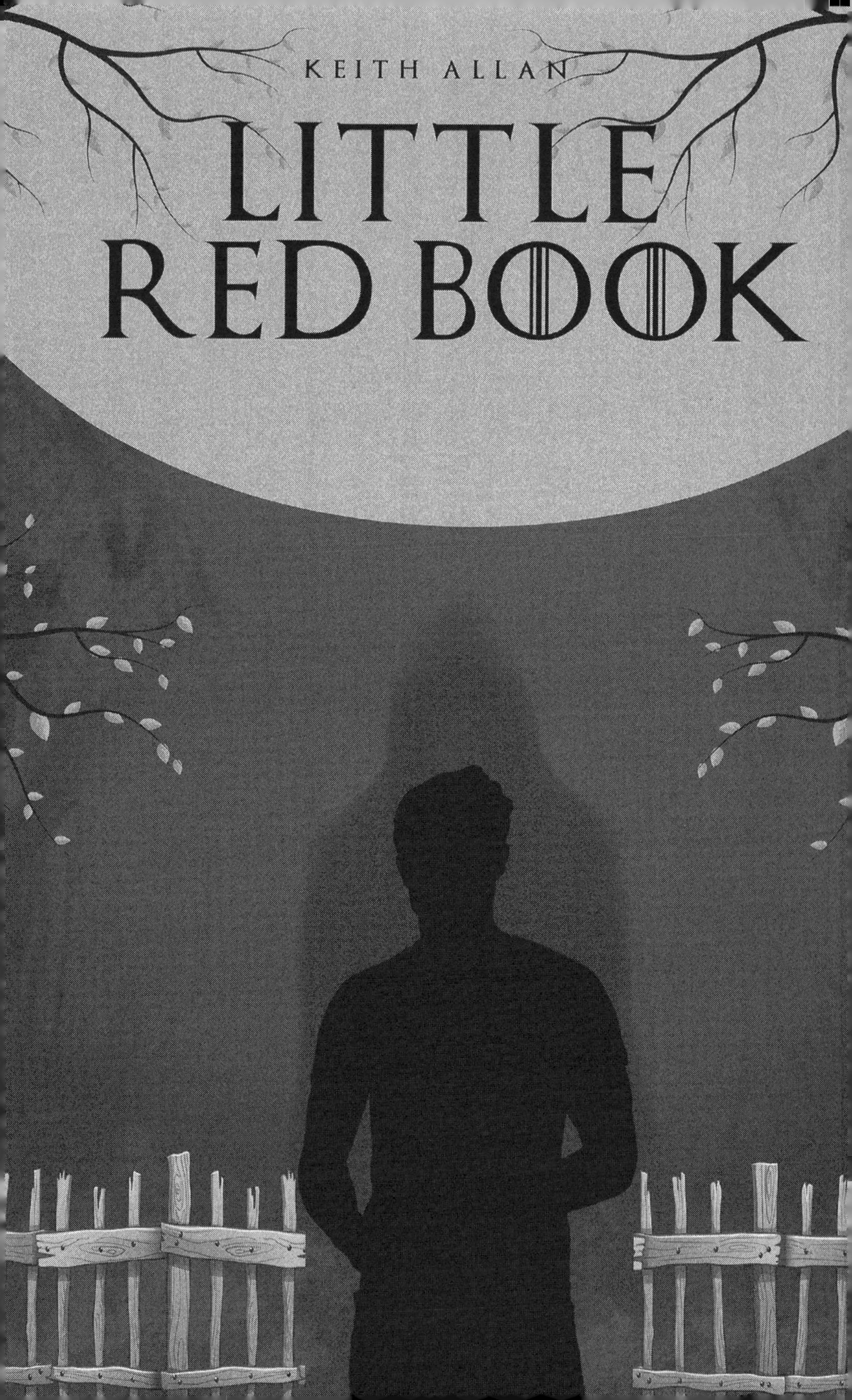
KEITH ALLAN
LITTLE
RED BOOK

Little Red Book

By

Keith Allan

Little Red Book

I'm Miller. Not pretty, not particularly smart, but I'm breathing. I'm an observer- I watch things. There's so much going down in LA, if you keep your eyes open you can make things happen. Right now I'm all about revenge. Two nights ago I jacked a car and headed for Vegas. I woke up in an alley behind some random strip club, with a bloody lip, a concussion, and a dancer named Whiskey's phone number written on the back of a bar napkin, along with the inscription "That was fun! Lol". Don't remember the fun part.

I used my last and best-stolen credit card (you don't keep the wallet, you lift it, remove the last credit card in the group, then return the wallet so the mark doesn't know anything is missing), to get a room at the Hard Rock. I bought some clothes, and began hunting down some asshole named Sanchez that burned me for ten grand on a coke deal in Hollywood the day before. Personally I hate the stuff, I've seen too many friends turn from Dr. Jekyll into Mr. Hyde, but I connected a buyer to a seller and was due my commission. My ex, tending bar downstairs, heard that my buddy Sanchez was working with some Russians, a group calling themselves the Collective, fencing stolen cars brought in from Miami. I don't like dealing with those guys, and was about to just say fuck it, when guess who I see across the club wooing some prospective clients? Yep, Sanny boy.

I quietly come up behind him, touch the back of his neck with my bowie knife, and announce to the gentlemen at the table that we have some unfinished business to attend to, and he'll be right back. Entering the bathroom, Sanchez tries to give me the slip, so I surgically removed his right ear during the struggle. As he's squirming on the blood drenched floor searching for his missing appendage, and whimpering like a little schoolgirl, I ask him about the ten grand. He says he only has four left, and hands me a wad of sticky bills. I give him a goal winning kick in the stomach, and tell him not to follow me- he still has one good ear (just love those cowboy boots with the steel toe). Common sense says I should leave town, but Cherie my ex mentioned there was a sucker's poker game going down at a little place out on the strip called Lulu's Love Palace. Sounds like a plan, so I head south through the scorching Vegas sun.

Lulu meets me in the lobby, along with a cadre of her finest- no shortage of silicon and five dollar perfume here. I ask her about the game, and she says it's a hundred to play, unless I want to spend some time with one or more of her employees later, then the game is free. I hand her a hundred, as a down payment, and tell her we'll see how the game goes.

She spins around towards the front desk and says," Christy, take Mr. Miller to the back room", to which I reply, "Its just Miller". Christy steps out from behind the counter, and I'm taken by her beautiful green eyes, and I have to take a breath. She's dreamy- petite, blond messy hair, wearing a sheer, sequin short dress unbuttoned in the front, revealing just enough to disturb my cool. She only glances up at me for a second at a time, and smiles at me as if she has a secret.

Lulu sees our connection, and breaks the moment with, "Christy's my niece, and she's not for sale." Christy grabs my hand and says, "come." She leads me to a long narrow hallway, with overhead lights every twenty feet or so, flickering and in need of repair. I hear grunts and groans from satisfied customers, the smell of sweat, sex, and some awful cleaning detergent, and it's hot as hell. I'm now following behind Christy. She occasionally looks back, smiles, and catches me looking below her waist.

She says, “Where are you from?”

“LA, the Hollywood area”, I reply.

“Really, I’ve always wanted to go there...take me?”

My first thought is hell yes! But I collect myself and say, “Are you an actress? How old are you?”

She replies, “No, I just like movie stars...I’m nineteen.”

“What brought you to Vegas?” I ask.

“ I hated Alabama, so I hitched out here and started working for Lulu, answering the phone, making appointments, shopping, whatever.” We reach the end of the hallway, she leans back against the wall, runs her index finger down her chest, leaving a path through the beads of sweat, slightly touching her right breast, then bringing her finger to her lips, “Damn its hot, don’t ya think?” Ok, I’m about to lose it, I want to drag her into any empty room, closet, or just go right there.

I regain a semblance of control, and tell her, “I’ve got to make some money, will you be here in a couple hours?”

“Of course, I’ll be right down the hall,” as she slightly widens her stance and points in the direction we came from with her right hand. She opens the door to her left, and points to a poker game in the back of a smoke filled room with her left hand.

As I enter I see three games going on, but I know which one is for me. Its got four players, three of which are suits that look like they flew into Vegas for a convention, a little cards and something else Lulu had to offer. The fourth guy is a player, he looks familiar, and so I’ll have to be careful with him. I introduce myself, they say hello, and welcome me at the table. The idea here is to go slow. Lose a little over the first hour, then slowly win a couple big hands, making it seem like you finally got lucky. I have few gifts, but I can remember what cards in a deck have been played, and I can pick up on people's body language.

After two hours I'm up about ten grand- it's time to manufacture an exit. This is the tricky part. There's security in the room, and I definitely don't want to deal with them inside the room or outside. I get a bit of luck when two of the suits announce they're done, so I chime in I've got to go too. As we get up from the table I hand a couple hundred to each of the bricks, and head for the exit. As I'm walking down the hall, I see Christy half way down leaning back smoking a cigarette.

"How'd ya do?" she asks.

"Good," I reply.

"Can you take me with you, I won't be any trouble...well, a little," she says with that seductive smile. "I'll just tell Lulu you're giving me a ride into town for groceries, and that I'll Uber back."

I'm powerless, "OK, let's go, but no promises." We run into Lulu in the front room. I hand her a stack of bills, "I did OK, but I've got to get back to the city". While she's flipping through the bills Christy explains the ride situation.

I'm looking at Lulu thinking by her facial expression she's not real thrilled with the idea, but her expression changes when she gets to the hundreds in the stack, "Yeah, yeah go ahead," she says and waves goodbye never looking up from her take. As Christy and I get in the car, I'm keeping a close eye on the surrounding area, hoping I paid off the right people enough to make a clean exit. As we pull away, I look over at Christy- she's smiling like a kid at Christmas, her head out the window, her hair blowing in the hot dry desert air. It's been a long day, and I need some rest. As we enter town I pull off the main streets and find a two-star rated hotel that'll do just fine. I park around back, keeping my car out of view from the street, just in case I've picked up a tail, or the Vegas PD spots my stolen car. I check in, hand Christy the room key, and tell her I'll be there in a minute; I'm going for some beer from the liquor store across the street.

When I get back to the room, I open the door she left slightly ajar. The room is dark except the light coming through the window across the room. Next to the window is a comfortable looking chair, and Christy is slouched down in it, naked, drinking a coke out of a bottle with a straw.

The fan in the window is blowing her hair, and she looks at me and says, "We could shower first, but I'd prefer we didn't." She's twirling her hair with one finger, then starts running her hand down the inside of her thigh. I'm no longer tired or thirsty I just want her. As I approach her she sits up and moves to the front edge of the chair, and using her index finger waves it at me motioning for me to get down. Still sipping on the coke, she places her other hand on the back of my head and guides me between her legs. This was probably the sexiest moment I've ever experienced, and it goes on for about two hours, us moving to the bed after her shuttering orgasms in the chair. I don't know what's in the water down in Alabama, but Jesus Christ, this girl rocked my world like no pro has ever done.

When it's finally over, we were like two balloons that flew around the room, deflated and spent to exhaustion. The white sheets were stained with sweat and body fluids, sticky and worn. After a couple of hours sleep I had a shower, opened a beer, and just sat back and enjoyed how the late afternoon sun played shadow games with her out stretched body. She slowly awakened, eased into her seductive smile, and motioned for me to join her. I sat on the bed next to her, wiped the hair from across her face, and suggested we should eat soon.

I told her about Sanchez and the Russians, and when I mentioned the Collective, she said she's seen them before, that they come to Lulu's every Thursday and throw money around. They like having more than one girl at a time, and even offered Lulu $5,000 for her. Much to her credit, Lulu refused, saying Christy was family and not on the menu. Christy said these guys had handfuls of cash, and came to Lulu's after their weekly dealings with some guys from Miami. I got her to tell me more, hoping there was a way to profit from these guys. She said it was the same every Thursday afternoon, they would call about 3:00, show up in a black Caddy, the driver would stand outside the car, one guy would go to the back of the car, open the trunk, get something out, what she couldn't see from the office window, then three guys came inside for the ladies. She described the three as a bunch of arrogant assholes that would often rough up the girls, and Lulu only put up with them because they paid double and triple the going rate. I asked her if she'd like to work a plan to get back at them and make some money. She said sure, she never liked those guys.

It was Wednesday, so we were only a day away. She showered; we drove into Vegas, bought her some new clothes, had dinner and saw a show. It was time for a new ride, so I dumped the Lexus and hot-wired an Audi that had been sitting for a while, judging by the dust layer and build up of debris in front of the tires. Just as a precaution I exchanged license plates with a car near by.

The next morning we had breakfast and finalized the plan. I called a buddy of mine in Vegas that deals in guns and knives. He sold me a modified German Glock 17, designed to shot tranquilizer darts. About two o'clock, we parked about a mile outside of Lulu's, at a truck stop. At 3:15, we saw the Caddy fly by, so we waited about a half hour to give the three guys time to pick their partners. Christy drove, I was lying down in the back seat. She pulled up parallel to the Caddy to its right. She was dressed in a super short red mini skirt, heals and black fishnets. She got out of the car, said hi to the driver and walked over to him. She asked him why he didn't get to have any fun, and ran her hand down the lapel of his jacket. We had left the backseat driver's side window down, so I slowly rose up and aimed at his back, as she kept him occupied. One shot would do it. The gun had a silencer on it so there wouldn't be much noise. I fired, hit him between the shoulder blades, and he arched his back, tried to reach behind him to remove the dart, but he crumpled to the ground unconscious. I quietly told Christy to pop the trunk as I exited the car and headed to the back of the Caddy. The trunk latch popped, and I lifted the hood.

I grabbed the black bag inside, told Christy, "Grab the keys and lets get the hell out of here". She ran back to the Audi, I stuck it in reverse, and then took off down the highway.

I told her, "Open the bag, lets see what's for Christmas!"

She opened it and said, "Oh my God!" and lifted out a few stacks of bills. We got back to the hotel, went inside, and poured out the contents of the bag. They were all hundred-dollar bills in each stack, and after a rough count it looked like close to $240,000.

I told her," Get your things together, were leaving for LA right now". We grabbed everything in sight, checked out of the hotel, and hit the road. We got back to LA around 9:00. My place wouldn't safe, so we got a cheap hotel on Sunset Blvd for the night.

By now, the Collective boys had probably put it together that Christy and I were the thieves, and running us down was top priority. I never tell anyone where I'm based; I always say I'm from the Bay area, so it might be a while before they head this way. The real concern is whether they speak with Sanchez. I've always done well playing cards in San Diego, my hometown, so that's our new destination.

As Christy rubs her eyes and smiles at the morning light streaking through the window, I hand her a Starbucks and kiss her on the forehead.

"Ever been to the beach?" I ask her.

"No, can we go? I use to watch movies about surfers and girls running down the beach...you know like Baywatch?". I tell her were going to buy a car, and get a place in La Jolla for a while, that's near San Diego. She jumps into my arms and says, "I can't believe it! This is the best day of my life!"

I pay cash for a used Mini Cooper, and we headed south. There's a cool apartment for rent above La Jolla cove, a place I actually lived at when I went to college at UCSD. After a little shopping, mostly bikinis, I give Ricky D., an old card playing buddy a call, and line up a game for that night. We purchase a couple pay per use phones, throw our old ones in the ocean, and grab some sushi.

Before heading to the game, I told Christy the new rules, "No contact with home, always pay cash, pick a new name you want to go by if someone asks, and if anyone asks my name is Jesse."

She said, "That's cool, um, I'll be Ginger!" acting as if this was just a game.

The game was at a nearby hotel, in a penthouse suite. I told Ricky in advance I was going by Jesse, and he introduced me as such to the players at the table. The buy in was $10,000, which was a little above my pay grade, but thanks to my fellow ruskies it wasn't a problem. The game had a predetermined end time, so I paced myself accordingly, so when 3:00am came around I'd be comfortably ahead. I was up about 40K at that point, and as I was about the leave I gave Ricky a couple grand, at which point he pulled me aside for a brief chat. He told me the Collective had nearly beaten Sanchez to death, thinking he was in on the heist with me. All he could tell them was where I lived in LA, so that place was surely trashed.

Ricky said "They're going to a lot of trouble for a quarter mill, they can sell two of their stolen lambos for that much money... you'd better watch your step."

Now I was getting nervous. I was thinking I was out of my league, in fact I was sure of it. Driving home I started considering leaving the country, someplace tropical would be nice. As I walked up the path to the apartment, I could see the front door was open. I looked around the perimeter of the building, but could see no one. I slowly opened the door, flicked on the light, and revealed a disaster reminiscent of a hurricane aftermath- and no Christy! Nailed to the wall was a note, and the Saint Christopher necklace she wore around neck. The note said, "Bring the bag and its contents in exchange for the girl, or she dies. Call 761-435-2007."

This was not good and getting worse. I could return the bag, I had the 240K, but how do I know they won't kill her, or me, at the exchange? I needed a plan, and I needed help from someone that would be familiar with this kind of thing.

I had placed the bag in a gym locker at a nearby fitness center, so the first thing was to see if it was still there. I went to the gym and thankfully it was. I checked into a local hotel, always making sure I wasn't followed. Once the I dumped out the money on the bed- all there. Then I noticed that at the bottom of the bag was a flat piece of hard plastic. I pulled it out and tapped to the underside was a red diary-size journal. I flipped through it and read some of the entries. It was a record of stolen cars, their pin numbers, and the names of the buyers. As I got towards the back there were some side notes and names of some Russian nationals.

It appeared as if a Demetri Kosovo was the journal owner, but there were also meeting times and places with a Boris Petroff. They didn't sound familiar, so I googeled them. Demetri is the lead counsel for Boris, who is the UN Ambassador to the United Nations! Holy shit! I'm not just over my head; I'm underwater about six fathoms! These guys are the Collective. Ok, so now I need some serious help.

Without giving any details, I call Ricky and see if he knows any people in the underworld, maybe special ops types or people with knowledge of hostage exchange. He knows this guy named Jason, ex seal, ex mercenary. He says I can call him and talk, but from this point on he wants nothing to do with it. I'm in completely unfamiliar territory now, and can only hope this guy can save me.

I give him a call. He agreed to meet with me at a coffee shop, but will discuss nothing over the phone. We meet the next morning at 11:00am. He's about 6'0 tall or so, built like a marine just out of boot camp, and has a short cropped beard with keen eyes. I'm 100% honest with him, because I get the feeling he could tell If I tried to be otherwise. He suggests we do the exchange in a very public place, I go alone, and he and his partner will oversee the exchange. It'll cost me 40K, a bargain for sure.

After some discussion about a location for the exchange, we decide on the Ellen Browning Park that borders the waterline adjacent to La Jolla Cove. Lots of tourist foot traffic, and good visibility from multiple angles. There's a six-story hotel across the street from the park, and the suites face the ocean. His partner will secure a sixth story suite, and the exchange will be visible from his vantage point. He's a former sniper with the Army Rangers. Upon hearing this I interrupt the discussion to insist no one is killed, and if it becomes necessary to use force, only shots to the arms and/or legs should be taken. He agrees, but says the situation will be fluid, and says things seldom go exactly according to plan- Christy's safety and mine are top priority. He will be on the ground, in disguise as a park custodian. He will arrive three hours prior to the exchange, and will give the go/no go a few minutes before the actual swap.

The plan seems doable, now I just need to get the Russians to agree to the time and place. It's time to give them a call. A person with a Russian or Ukrainian accent answers.

Hello", to which I reply, "This is Miller."

"We meet tomorrow, you get girl, I get bag."

"I need to meet in a public place, of my choice. I will keep the money, but will bring the book. These terms are not negotiable. "

He says," How bout I just kill the girl!".

"Fine, I don't know her that well anyway. I'll take the book to the FBI."

"Okay, we meet like you want."

"Tomorrow at 11:00am, at the Ellen Browning Park. There's a bench overlooking the water at the west most end of the park. It will have a red paint stripe across its back. I will be sitting there, so when you arrive walk in front of me with the girl. I get the girl, you get the book. No other people or I walk to the nearest police officer."

"Okay, we do it your way." and hangs up.

I confirm with Jason, give him the 40K, and he sets things in motion. He will carry a tranquilizer gun and a tazer, and will subdue any extra personnel from interfering with the exchange. He seems legit, and I trust Ricky with his recommendation- not like I have other options. I'm a big believer of having a plan B, and in this case I need to come up with a way I can insure Christy and my safety once the exchange is made. Here's what I'm thinking might work. I'll make three photocopies of the book. I have an old college buddy that practices criminal law in San Diego. I'll take the copies to him with instructions that I will check-in with him weekly, at a specified day of the week, and time of the day. Should I fail to do so, he will send the copies to three people- the president of the UN Security Council, and the editors of the New York Times and the Washington Post. I'll build in contingencies, but this is the basic plan. I'll leave a note describing what will happen inside the book, so the Russians are aware that killing Christy or myself will lead to severe consequences to the Collective, and the political future of the UN Ambassador.

I drive to San Diego, and meet with my lawyer friend. He wants to insure that he is not complicit in the exchange, and though we can invoke attorney client privilege, he wants assurances that he in no way was aware of exchange and what led up to it. I minimize the details of what has happened, and assure him his role is strictly concerned with receiving my weekly contact, and carrying out the distribution of the copies. He agrees to the plan, with some understandable reluctance.

Over the next few hours, I start thinking about how many ways this can go sideways. I'm mostly concerned with Christy's safety. She is young and has had little to do with what's transpired over the last few days. This is on me. Looking back, I should have just let her alone and left Lulu's alone. But now I need to focus on the present- our only way out of this is to carry out the plan, and pray things work out.

It's morning. Jason has secured a parking spot for me a brief walk from the exchange location. I'm to walk quickly to my car with Christy, and drive out of town. If everything goes well, I will never speak to Jason again, which is fine with me. Right now I just want distance from this whole cluster-fuck. If there is gunfire or some other altercation, I have to keep it together and get us out of there.

I arrive at the park at 10:40. I park my car and walk into the park. It's a clear day, and there are a variety of people enjoying the day, walking about, going down to the water, and unaware of what's about to go down. As I walk down the cement path that surrounds the large park, I see Jason with a broom and a handheld dustpan, the type you see grounds people using collect small amounts of trash and debris. I also notice a couple men that seem somewhat out of place, dressed in dark clothes, trousers, and in general unseasonable attire. Jason has been sweeping up since 8:00, I'm sure he's spotted the potential problems. I see the bench ahead, and the red stripe painted on its backside. Its about 10:50 when I sit down on the bench. There's no sign of Christy and her escort. Jason gave me an earpiece to communicate between the three of us, and said he might give instructions during the exchange and the few minutes following. I learned later, in a text from Jason, that Jason's partner, let's call him James, saw a black sedan park a half hour before the exchange, and two men got out and positioned themselves about a hundred yards on either side of the exchange point- one sitting on a bench to the south and the other walking about along the cement pathway to the north.

At about 11:05, James notified Jason and myself that a man and a young woman left the car, and were walking my way. A few minutes later, Christy and the man appeared as instructed in front of me. James told me to get up and move to the right of Christy and her escort. As I positioned myself, I asked Christy if she was okay. She nodded yes, but she looked stressed out and scared. James told me to hold up my right hand, with my palm facing the park. As I did, a red laser light appeared on my palm. The Russian immediately noticed this.

I said, "I only want the girl, here's the book." The book was sealed with two rubber bands, wrapped around from top to bottom, and left to right. The Russian took a quick look at the book, grabbed it out of my hand, and shoved Christy towards me, and then walked north.

As he stared at the book, I yelled out "Read page 51!" He looked at me somewhat confused, but continued walking.

I started walking south when I heard James say exchange made. I was approaching the Russian on the bench, who had just stood up. Jason came in from behind him and tazed the back of his neck, catching the man from behind and sitting him back on the bench.

Jason said, " R1 subdued".

At this point James said "R2 aware, headed your way." The Russian that had been positioned along the pathway to the north, tagged R2, had joined the exchange escort, but was now running towards us. Jason had stepped behind a utility building, taking himself out of view from the approaching man. At this point I told Christy we've got to get out of here, taking her hand and nearly running back towards my car. As R2 rounded the utility building, Jason shot the man in the thigh with the tranquilizer gun. R2 stumbled for a few feet, and then collapsed. I looked back to see a few people coming to the aid of the fallen man, but we continued quickly to the car.

I heard James say "Car driver exited vehicle, and is in pursuit of client...I've got him." We reached the sidewalk that leads to the car, when I heard a faint pop. I turned around and saw the driver on the ground holding his leg, and a pistol he had been holding lying in the street.

We got to the car as I fumbled for my keys. I was shaking at this point, but we jumped in and got it started. I zoomed by the crippled driver, and we drove away.

I looked at the visibly shaken Christy and said" Are you okay babe? I'm so sorry for this, were gunna make it." I know the area, so we got out of La Jolla and headed south. "Ricky got us clean passports and ID's. I've got a poker buddy that owns a hotel in Mexico right on the beach. We can catch a flight out of San Diego. Want to go to Tulum?" She smiled and jumped over to my seat, laying her head on my shoulder.

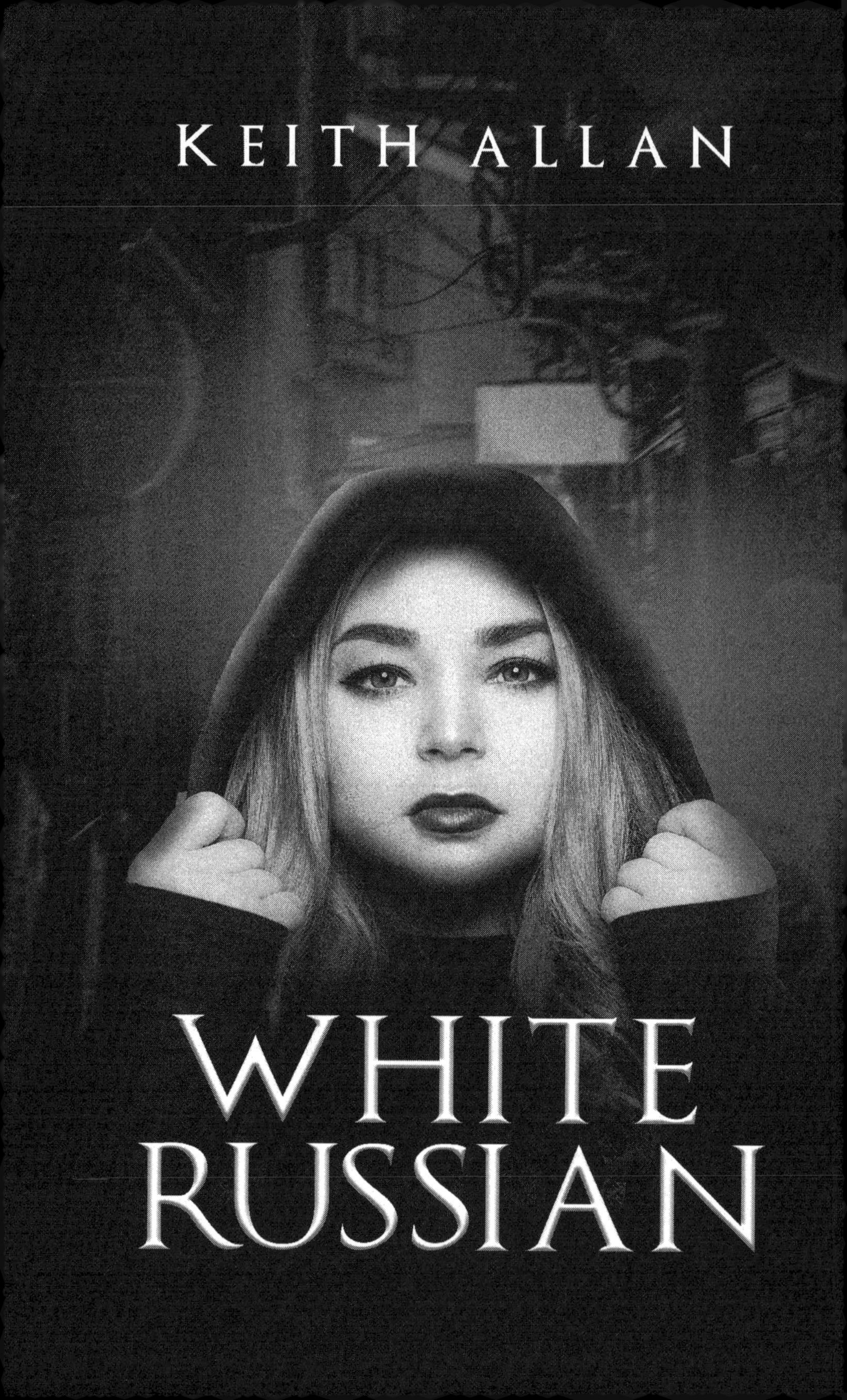
KEITH ALLAN
WHITE
RUSSIAN

White Russian

By

Keith Allan

White Russian

"A White Russian, please."

I had just come out of the back and hadn't seen her come in. She sat at the end of the bar dressed in a black hoodie and loose-fitting cargo pants and was sitting in the dark just outside of the bar lights.

"Sure thing," I said, glancing up and making brief eye contact. As I prepared her drink, it reminded me of an encounter I had about a year ago in Prague when a contact called me a White Russian. My father was from St. Petersburg, so I grew up speaking English and Russian. The CIA recruited me out of college, with a major in international business. A few years of servitude convinced me that the life of an operative was not for me.

She pulled back her hoodie. "You're René, right? René Sinclair?" she said in a muted tone.

"Yes, have we met?" Now I could see her facial features: kind of a narrow, defined jawline, green eyes, and no makeup.

"I think you know my brother, Mike Broderick?" she replied.

I hadn't heard that name in a couple years, but Mike was a stand-up guy and a good soldier.

"Yeah, Mike and I worked together overseas, great guy."

"He said you two were kind of close and I could count on you to be discreet."

This set off an alarm. I wasn't sure what was coming, but at this point I had a few questions of my own.

"How did you find me?" I said.

"I just want a few minutes of your time. I want to show you something . . . it's important," she said, ignoring my question.

"I'm a bartender now and don't work for the company anymore. I'm a civilian." What's important to her, may not be to me. I'd seen enough of "important" and was over trying to change the world. I just wanted a semi-normal existence. Mike had my back in some tough situations, though, so I decided to give her a listen. "But okay, just not here. There's a coffee shop on Third Avenue called the Morning Buzz. Let's meet there in the morning, say eleven o'clock?"

"I know it, perfect, see you then," and with that, she got up and walked out.

The next morning, I was running through various scenarios in my head, none of which had favorable outcomes. I'm not a strong-arm, and I'm not interested in bleeding for a cause. I figured a few years in the intelligence field in service to our country was enough. Besides, I worked in foreign affairs, not domestic issues. Well, I might be overthinking the whole thing; I've done that before.

As I walked into the coffee shop, I saw her sitting at a small table in the back. She was dressed in a running outfit, and I must admit, she was much better looking than Mike. But no matter what she had to say, I wasn't going to let her looks affect the outcome of our meeting. I ordered a small coffee and took it to her table. She had some green, awful-looking health drink that could have been blended weeds.

"Hi" I said, as I sat down.

"Good morning," she said. "I hate to drag you into this, but I don't know what else to do."

"What can I do for you?"

"I work for a marketing company and was recently at an international marking symposium in Vancouver, BC. On the last day, I met a guy at a hospitality event, and regretfully, ended up sleeping with him that night. I woke up the next morning around nine, and he was gone. He left a note saying he had to be at the airport early, and loved meeting me. I checked out of my hotel and drove home around eleven. The next day, I got a call from the Seattle police, asking if I was aware of the break-in that occurred at 4167 West Dorn Street in Seattle. That's my previous address, where I'd lived with my ex-husband. I told them I haven't lived there for a couple months, since the divorce. They said the house was ransacked and they found a note that said, 'Sarah, call me, Todd.' Todd was the guy I slept with. I'm sorry to bother you, but I'm scared and don't know what to do."

He was obviously looking for something, but what? "Have you looked through your luggage, or any items you took with you to the conference?"

"Yes, everything is there, nothing missing."

"How about your car? I assume you drove?"

"I didn't really check it, but it seems like it's the same."

"Let's go check."

We walked outside and over to her car. It was a very generic Toyota Corolla. She unlocked it, and I started scouring the inside. This involved checking everything—the seats, under the dash, and the side panels—to see if it looked like they had been removed and returned. Nothing. "Pop the trunk." It was empty, so I removed covering where the spare is kept. Bingo. There was a large heavy-plastic bag, about the size of a bag of fertilizer. It was vacuum-packed and sealed tight on all ends. I carry a pocketknife, so I cut into it. Inside were several clear plastic bags containing some orange triangular pills. I cut into one of those bags and removed a pill. It had little smell, and touching it to my tongue revealed nothing. I had a feeling for what it was, but I didn't want to alarm Sarah, so I just muttered, "Huh."

After a moment, I asked, "Where are you staying now?"

"I have a flat in downtown Tacoma."

"I'm going to check this out, but as a precaution, I think you should not go back there. I have some people at the Seattle field office that can identify what this is. I don't suppose you have any info on this guy, or a photo?"

"I might have a photo." She took out her phone, and she found one photo with him in a group shot of a bunch of conference attendees toasting at the mixer. There were people in the foreground, so I'm guessing he didn't realize she had photographed him.

"Until we can figure out who this guy is, we'd better assume he has some ability to track you down, so here's what I suggest. You need to ditch your phone—you can take out the memory card, but throw away the body. Let me see your driver's license and passport." She handed them to me. "These have your old address. Was there anything else in your purse or baggage that has your current address?"

"No," she said. "About a month ago I changed my name back to my birth name, because my ex was abusive and I didn't want him to find me."

"Okay, these next steps are not going to be easy, but we've got to hide you for a while. Go into Seattle to a branch of your bank and take out a thousand dollars. Call your workplace and tell them you need a week off, maybe say it's a family emergency or something. Buy a pay-per-use phone and call me when you get it. Langley gave me an untraceable number when I left the agency, so we can communicate."

"No problem."

"Buy any items you might need for, let's say, a week. You know, sundries, change of clothes, those kinds of things. Don't use any credit cards or anything electronic; don't call any friends or relatives. Here's my address and phone number. When you get back from Seattle, I'm going to put you up in a hotel in my name, here in town. We can put your car in my space at my apartment complex to keep it off the streets."

At this point, I could tell she was kind of freaking out. I needed to remember this was a world I was familiar with, but to her, it was a trip to Mars. I put my arm around her shoulder and tried to calm her down. "Look, I know this is crazy stuff, but we can get through this. I just need you safe until I figure out how deep the rabbit hole goes.

"I'm going up to the Seattle field office. I've got some ins there that can help with this. Text me that photo. I'm going to take the pills with me for analysis, and with the photo maybe we can identify this guy. As soon as you get the new phone, call me."

I drove up to the Seattle field office, and the receptionist called an old acquaintance of mine, Paul McDonald. "Paul said come on up. The elevator is to your right, and he's on the fourth floor, room 419."

When I got to his office, he was waiting at the door. "I never thought I'd see you again! How have you been?" he said.

"Pretty good. I sleep well now," I said and chuckled. We both went in, and he sat down behind his desk while I took a seat in front of him.

"Coming back to work? We could use a smart guy around here, and I could use someone to drink with."

"No, but I do have something you could help me with." I explained the situation and handed him one of the pills. "Is this what I think it is?"

He examined it and pushed a button on his phone. "Jamie, come in here, please." When his secretary came in, he put the pill in a small plastic bag and handed it to her. "Take this to the lab for analysis, and tell them I need to know right away." After she left, he asked me, "Where'd you get it?"

"A friend drove them across from Vancouver. She got played and some guy hid them in the trunk of her car. I've got a few thousand of them in my car. Like a fertilizer-sized bag of them. I'm parked in the lot, space 43. You're welcome to them; they're in the back seat, it's unlocked." Paul told a couple of agents to go retrieve them. "I want to find out who this guy is and get him off the street. Here's a recent photo of him. It's the guy in the black shirt and white tie." I sent him a text of the photo. He forwarded it to a forensic lab where they do facial recognition.

"We should know pretty quick. If he's Canadian, that narrows down the search. I'll call you in a couple hours; we should hear from both labs by then. It's getting near noon, so can I buy you some lunch? The food here is pretty decent, actually."

"Sure, sounds good."

After lunch, we traded stories for a while. As we were leaving the cafeteria, he got a call from Jamie. The labs had checked in. We went back to his office and his boss, the director of the branch, joined us there. "Justin Peters," he said, as he extended his hand.

"René Sinclair," I replied.

There was a large screen on the wall opposite Paul's desk, where photos and bio summaries were displayed. "Our guy's real name is Raul Diamond. He's a Canadian national. A couple busts for drug possession, arrested for smuggling once but wasn't convicted. He's currently in the employ of Novak Pharmaceuticals. Says he's a sales rep. They manufacture oxycodone and a couple other pain-relief products. We've had our eyes on them for a while. They've been selling oxy to US distributors, a couple of which are currently under indictment for illegal sales. That pill was fentanyl. We need to shut this place down. Manufacturing and/or distributing illegal drugs has eluded us in regard to Novak, so we need something solid.

"I read your file, René, and your history and skill set are perfect for this. I'd like to deputize you as a temporary agent, just for this case. We can provide all services available to full-time agents, and we'll make sure you and Sarah are well compensated for your efforts. We're going after Novak, and Raul is just icing on the cake. We believe they're producing fentanyl, not just distributing it from overseas sources. Our hope is to catch Raul in a sting operation and offer him a plea deal if he assists us in going after Novak."

Throughout his discourse, I had a feeling this was coming, and I'm sure my facial expressions and body language were telling. "I'm a civilian now, and stepping into this world again means revisiting the dark side of society. A world I want to avoid."

"I understand. Opioids are now the most addictive drug in America, and fentanyl is the new heroin, killing thousands upon thousands. But this would be a one-time thing. We could really use you. Your country could really use you."

I'd been waiting for the patriotic appeal.

"I'll see what kind of a plan we can develop," I said, "but no promises. If it doesn't look right, I'm out."

"Fair enough. We'll set you up with an office near Paul's, and we can start right away. Were honored to have you on the team, and we'd like you to be the team leader." He held out his hand, we shook, and he left Paul's office.

"Here we go! Glad to have you aboard!" Paul said. I'm sure that was said to the passengers boarding the Titanic.

"See you in the morning," I replied, and I left the office.

It was time to get a place in Seattle for a couple of days. I got back to my car when the phone rang; it was Sarah.

"He came to my work!" she said in a panic-stricken voice. "The receptionist called me and said a guy came in, claiming to be my cousin. He knew a few things about me, so she believed him. She gave him my new number!"

"Okay, we need to relocate you in case he can track your phone. Smash the phone, grab your stuff, and get out of there. I'm getting a hotel room in Seattle for a few days. I'll get a two-bedroom suite and you can stay with me. Take an Uber to Seattle, and by the time you get there I should have it ready. Remember to pay cash for the Uber driver and offer the driver an extra $50 to keep it off the books. We've opened the case at the CIA and are developing a plan. Don't panic, you'll be safe with me."

I found a place. Sarah got a new phone and called me. I had her meet me at a restaurant near the hotel. She looked relieved to see me, and ran up and gave me a desperate hug. She was shaking and kept my embrace for a few seconds. "It's okay, I got you. We're just down the street. Are you hungry? We can grab a bite."

We had dinner and walked to the hotel. "Are you a wine drinker?" I asked.

"Yes, definitely!" she replied. We picked out a bottle at a liquor store just beyond the hotel and made our way back and up to the suite. I figured the wine would help calm her nerves, and I could use a glass myself.

We had grown close in the short time we'd known each other, so sharing a hotel room wouldn't be difficult. But I had to keep this strictly platonic. Once you mix business with pleasure, your mind gets cloudy and your decision-making takes a hit. This was a bit of a test for me. She was an attractive lady and somewhat vulnerable, but I'd seen this movie before, and it was up to me to keep disciplined.

She drank the majority of the wine and passed out on the couch. I carried her to her room, laid her on the bed, and threw a cover over her.

In the morning, I caught her up on the situation, leaving out certain details that weren't necessary for her to know. I told her to stay in the room and order room service for food, and that I would call her in a couple hours. She seemed much more at ease now, so I left for the headquarters.

When I arrived, Paul greeted me and showed me to my office. "We have a meeting at ten o'clock in my office. See you then." We needed to catch Raul with the fentanyl in order to make an arrest stick. I'd been thinking about a way to do that all night. A few minutes before ten, I made my way over.

There were a couple of extra agents in the room besides the director, Paul, and me. "You're lead on this, René. Let's hear from you first. By the way, how's the woman holding up?" Justin asked.

"She's good. Okay, we need to get Raul out in the open. Sarah will need to call Raul and set things up, but I want her away from the area when he arrives. She needs to act like she doesn't know what he really wants, but she wants free of it all, and he can have whatever it is. I suggest a public parking lot with a limited number of exits. She parks the car at a designated time, leaves it unlocked, and walks away. We cover her the whole way. It needs to look like the drugs have not been discovered, so we replace the large bag in her trunk. Let's seal it up tight and patch the slit I made. Place the bag slit-side down in the spare-tire compartment. If everything goes well, we can move in once he's transferred the bag to his vehicle. We need him alive, so our team and snipers need to know, no head or kill shots."

This plan seemed agreeable to the team, so the next step was to find a good location and work out the logistics: exit and entrance routes, sniper positions, number and types of vehicles, streets to block off, contingency plans, etc. We would have to bring Sarah in for the phone call and prep her on what to say, how to act, and most important, how to choose a location that is doable on our end and acceptable to Raul.

After developing all the details, I left the office and headed back to the hotel. I explained the basic plan to Sarah, and we went through the key points she would need to bring out, so her conversation with Raul would go according to plan. She seemed receptive and eager to do her part. We did a few mock phone calls, where I played the role of Raul.

We ordered room service and watched a movie. I could feel that we were getting to be close friends, and at some point, we might have a physical relationship. After a few glasses of wine, I relayed to her how important it was to focus on our task, and how a more involved relationship right now might cloud our judgment, as emotions often do. She was going through a lot at that point, so no need to add to the mix.

After the movie, I suggested I was getting tired and was ready for bed, and she agreed. As she walked to her room, I followed her to close the door behind her. She turned abruptly and put a hand on the back of my neck, and we kissed.

"Good night, René."

"Good night."

In the morning, we drove to the headquarters. A meeting was set for 9:00 a.m., and new to the team were a couple of CIA agents, there to provide cover, vehicles, and advice on location and traffic information. I introduced Sarah to the team and we again reviewed the direction of her upcoming conversation with Raul. As we rehearsed the phone-call scenarios, the team was visibly impressed with her responses to their "What if he says this?" questions.

We developed a list of four possible locations and went through positions for various members of the team and action plans. If he insisted on a location, we would pull up a map and give Sarah a thumbs up or thumbs down. She would have to give a reason why a certain location wouldn't work for her, like she didn't know where it was, or wasn't familiar with the area.

It was time to call. They gave everyone ear buds so we could listen in on the conversation.

She punched in the number. After a few rings, he answered.

"Hello?"

She replied, "It's Sarah from the symposium. I got your note to call. The police said you or someone ransacked my old house. Why did you do that?" Her tone was perfect, a mix of nervousness and naïveté.

"You have something of mine. I can't say what, but it's in your car."

"There's nothing in my car; I keep it pretty clean."

"It's there. Let's meet somewhere and I'll remove it. I'm sorry about your place, it's just very important I recover what's in your car. I mean you no harm, and once I get the item, I'll leave you alone, I promise."

"Okay, but I'm scared and don't want to see you again."

"No problem. You can park the car and leave it unlocked, and I'll take out my item and walk away."

"Well, I guess that's okay. Um, how about if I park in the Westfield Mall parking lot?"

"No, park in the lot in back of the Blue Parrot nightclub."

"Where's that? I think I'd feel better about a more public place."

There was a long pause. "The Coaster parking lot off Fourth Street."

We quickly pulled it up on the screen. It looked doable, so we wrote on a piece of paper, "the north lot." She answered, "Okay, that's fine, I catch the train there. I'll park in the north lot."

"Good. You park at 3:00 and I'll be there at 3:15."

"Okay, I'll be there."

The CIA crew immediately sent an agent to the lot. A high-altitude drone was dispatched, and within minutes, we had a clear view of the area. At the very furthest point north, there were very few cars; it was basically an overflow area that was seldom used. We could see a few scattered cars, but the row we were interested in was adjacent to a field, and there were no cars parked there now. We picked a space for Sarah to park in. That lot had only one real entrance and exit, making it ideal, in case an attempt to flee was made. The team sketched out the various positions the support team would take and a plan for how things would go down.

Sarah would park at 2:55 and walk to the train station. I would catch her eye at the train station and follow her as she walked through. She would go to the second floor and go to the restroom. Two undercover agents would guard the entrance. Once Raul arrived, he would be given just enough time to transfer the bag into his car. Then the CIA would converge with three vehicles to trap and block any attempt to escape from the area. We also would be getting additional support from the DEA for the duration of the operation, including personnel and intelligence.

Various contingencies were discussed and planned for. An older van would be parked about fifty feet away, with armed agents inside. The van was already on its way and would just wait around until it was time. We had to assume that Raul would soon observe the area, so the van needed to appear like it had been there for a while, maybe for days. Snipers would be positioned on the roof of a storage building a couple hundred yards away and were instructed to shoot out the tires of Raul's car, should he get as far as the driver's side and attempt to drive away.

I drove back to Tacoma to get Sarah's car. She joined me, and we drove my car and hers to the headquarters. Upon arrival, a couple of agents met us in the rear lot and placed the bag in the spare-tire compartment. For the next few hours, Sarah and I hung out in my office. She seemed calm enough, considering the events about to take place. I tried to keep the mood light. I could feel an underlying nervous energy in the room, so I mixed humor and unrelated stories into the conversation. I told her everything would be over soon, and with Raul in custody she could return to her life, and I could go back to pouring drinks and listening to people's problems and aspirations.

We timed it so she would arrive on schedule. There was little activity in the lot, and she parked in the space we had planned for. I was already up on the second floor of the station and had a distant view of her arrival. She parked and immediately started walking toward the station. I saw her enter, and as she walked toward the stairs she saw me and gave a little smile but kept going, walking up the stairs and into the bathroom. At that point, I returned to my observation point to see how things would unfold.

At 3:14, a gray van slowly entered the lot. It drove around the lot's perimeter twice and finally parked next to Sarah's car. Sarah was parked parallel to the curb, and the van pulled in to the space behind her. With binoculars, I could make out Raul as the driver.

The back doors of the van opened, and two men jumped out and walked over in front of Sarah's car. They were pros and appeared to have body armor on and Uzi-like automatic guns in their right hands. They looked from left to right, surveying the area.

This wasn't going to go down easy. Finally, Raul got out and went straight for the trunk. I could see him bent over, evidently opening up the spare-tire compartment. He walked the bag to the rear of the van, threw it in, and climbed into the driver's seat.

At that moment, the CIA van doors opened and three armed agents jumped out, already pointing their guns at the two gunmen. I could hear a megaphone saying, "This is the CIA. Drop your weapons, step forward, and get on the ground."

The gunmen instantly started firing. The CIA agents took cover behind their van and returned fire. One of the gunmen went down, and as the other tried to get to the back of the van, he too was hit and fell to the ground. There were now three armored vehicles closing in on the van. I heard the high-pitched sound of a sniper rifle, and the front and rear driver-side tires of the van went flat. Raul had started the van, backed up a little, then started to drive away, but was immediately blocked in by the approaching armored vehicles.

Next, I heard, "Get out of the vehicle with your hands up. There's nowhere to go. This is your only warning." Raul got out, and after a couple of steps, he was instructed to lay down on the ground with his hands behind him. He did so, and two agents immediately placed him in handcuffs and stood him up.

I ran over to the ladies' room where Sarah was waiting and went inside, and she ran to my arms as I was saying, "It's over, it's over."

An ambulance arrived shortly and attended to the downed gunmen. In my earpiece I could hear, "All clear, close the lot and send in the K7 team," indicating the cleanup crew.

As we walked out of the station, I turned to Sarah and said, "Ride with me; your car will be impounded. You'll be getting a new one."

She looked at me a bit surprised, then said, "Oh well, it was a dog anyway."

We laughed, and I drove us back to headquarters. There was a short debriefing, and toward the end of it, I interjected, "I'm taking Sarah home. Great work, everyone." She had waited in my office during the debriefing, so on the way back to the hotel, I explained how the operation went, leaving out a few unpleasant details.

At the hotel, both of us mentally and emotionally drained, we agreed a dinner out was in order. We both wanted showers, and she insisted I go first. A couple minutes into my shower, the bathroom door opened, then the shower door. She said, "We can save water if we shower together." With that, she hugged me, laying her head against my chest. After a few seconds, she looked up at me, and we kissed as the water streamed down our heads. After a few more seconds, she grabbed a bar of soap and said, "Let's get you clean," soaping my chest and looking up at me with a seductive smile. I flipped her around and pressed her against the glass shower wall, putting my arms around her and enclosing her breasts. She moaned as I kissed her neck, letting my hands slide down below her waist. With my right hand I pushed open the shower door, and she stepped out and turned around. I picked her up under her arms and she wrapped her legs around my waist. I carried her to my bed and we fell together.

After about two hours, we got dressed and went to dinner. Over dinner, I explained to her that I would be needed for the next phase of the operation. It was difficult to tell how long this next phase would last; I was hoping only a week or so. I would most likely be in Vancouver. The CIA wanted to sequester Sarah until the operation was completed, in case Raul's associates tried to find her. I convinced them to let her stay with me at a safe house just outside of the city. This was a hard sell, but I told them it was a condition I insisted upon for my continued involvement in the operation.

The next morning, I drove to headquarters for a meeting with the team that would be handling the next phase of the operation. The agent in charge of logistics outlined the physical layout of Novak Pharmaceuticals.

"We have confirmed that Novak has been purchasing LAH, which is a chemical compound used as a reducing agent in the production of synthetic fentanyl. The facility is located in a somewhat isolated area on the east end of Vancouver. One way in and one way out. Here's a view of the building and surrounding grounds." He put the ground-floor overhead view, from the architects plans submitted to the city, on the screen.

"In the back of the building, you can see two separate structures, listed as storage units." He put another image on the screen. "Now you see an infrared image taken by a high-altitude surveillance drone. About twenty yards behind the second storage unit, you can see a what appears to be a heat bloom, which we are guessing is coming from an underground structure, possibly a ventilation conduit. We believe this is the lab where the fentanyl is produced. There is a power box on the north side of storage unit two.

"We need to gain access to the underground lab and control any video systems, motion detectors, or possible alarm systems from there. We have permission from the Vancouver City Police to create an electrical malfunction affecting the entire building, giving us a reason to send out a repair team using a Vancouver Electric

Authorities vehicle. The repair crew should be able to identify what systems are in place and tap in to take control when necessary."

At this point the director stepped in. "We want to send in two agents at night. We will deactivate any alarm systems on the grounds. The goal is to find the entrance to the lab via the second storage unit, enter, and send out visual evidence of the lab and its purpose. Once this is received and confirmed, we'll raid the grounds and secure any personnel present. In about an hour, we will be questioning Raul and hopefully adding some clarity and details to the grounds and finding out specifically what he knows about the lab. Let's go on hold for a couple hours, and we'll reconvene after the interrogation."

We were called together later that afternoon to the director's office. He addressed the group. "We offered Raul a plea deal, promising him reduced charges and jail time, depending upon the value of what he gave us. Here's what we got: He's been in the lab, and it is accessed through the second storage unit. There's a sliding panel at the back of the lab, opened by a switch hidden under a shelf. Once the panel is opened, there's a metal door, which can only be opened with an ID card and fingerprint scanner. We have his card and are making a synthetic thumb skin using his print.

"There are guards walking the perimeter of the grounds 24/7. We will be able to track their positions with thermal imaging provided by our drone. One agent will enter the lab, and one will be positioned outside the storage unit in cover. It's unknown if an entrance to the lab will be relayed to the guards, but they do wear earbuds, so we should assume this will happen. It's therefore important that the agent inside acts quickly.

"Again, once we are sent digital evidence that the lab is producing fentanyl, our vehicles will enter the compound to secure the area and personnel. We have a helicopter on standby just outside the grounds, in case it's needed. René, we want you inside the lab. Agent Carmichael"—pointing to his left—"will be your partner. We've brought in a tech that's familiar with what to look for in the lab. He'll bring René up to speed." He motioned to the computer tech. "Can you bring up the satellite view of the grounds?"

He continued. "There are motion detectors surrounding the lab area. We should be able to disable them. You two will enter through the woods, which surround the area. Here's the drop point, about a quarter of a mile from the compound. You'll be coming in from the rear of the storage units, here." He pointed to the drop point and scrolled along the screen, defining a route to the units.

"We will disable the building's electrical system tomorrow morning. The repair crew will arrive shortly afterward. If they are able to identify what we need to know and how to operate their systems remotely, the operation will take place at 1:00 a.m. tomorrow night. Okay, let's break and split up into our sub-teams. René, stick around for a minute."

As the room cleared, I took a seat in front of the director's desk. "A couple more things we learned from Raul," the director said. "He had a tattoo on his left sleeve." He showed me a photo. "He's part of a smuggling gang known as 'The Inquisition.' These guys are bad news, responsible for numerous assassinations in southern Canada and the US. He also said that Sarah was on their watch list. I just wanted you to know."

"Thanks."

"Of course," he replied, and I left his office.

I met up with Carmichael at an operations prep room and we finalized what equipment we would need. We talked about similar missions we'd been involved in, and he seemed quite well suited for our job. We were to meet at headquarters at 11:00 p.m. There would be continual surveillance of the area from a proprietary satellite scanning in infrared to detect any people on the grounds. All team members would be able to speak and hear each other, and I would set up a hot spot at the entrance to the lab to ensure transmission to and from. Contingency plans had been developed, and the Canadian authorities had authorized the use of deadly force if deemed necessary. They were very cooperative and wanted a successful result as much as we did. Smuggling across the border had become a priority target, as well as a political hot topic, for law enforcement, and they would like to take credit for participating in a major bust. On our side, cooperation with our northern neighbors was always a priority, a sign of goodwill between the two countries.

That afternoon, I returned to the safe house. Sarah was able to work remotely through a secure network within the building. She seemed to be comfortable in her new surroundings, and we ordered food from the house chef. The CIA had brought in extra support staff, and though the room provided was windowless, it was well furnished and adequate for a short stay. I filled in the major details of the operation. She was very concerned with my safety, but I told her not to worry, that it was a piece of cake. Wishful thinking on my part.

At about 10:30, I went back to headquarters. The electrical repair team gave the operation the green light, having successfully tapped into the video, motion, and electrical systems in the lab as well as the surrounding grounds. After gearing up, we were driven to the drop point.

A tall chain-link fence surrounded the compound. Carmichael used a hydrogen spray to freeze an opening in the fence. At this point, we received confirmation that the area motion sensors had been disabled and the video cameras on the interior of the lab had been frozen, displaying the last image recorded. We made our way through the forested area, aided by the use of night-vision goggles. Command was tracking the movement of the guards, and once we neared the storage units, we waited until it was clear. Getting a "Go!" I used a pressure punch on the door lock and entered the unit. Carmichael found a position behind some crates outside the unit and gave the all clear. I found the switch that opened the sliding panel leading to the lab entrance (thanks, Raul). As we were told, there was another door with a keycard reader and fingerprint scanner (again, thanks, Raul). I applied the synthetic thumb skin and slid the card through the reader, and the door popped open.

A somewhat-lit stairway took me down a narrow hallway to the lab. I pulled a room-filling light from my backpack and scanned the room for possible booby traps or unforeseen sensors. I could clearly see the equipment that I had been briefed on by the chem-tech, and I began photographing and sending several images. There were containers filled with the same types of pills we had confiscated. The evidence was undeniable, so it was time to exit.

As I was leaving, I saw some photographs on a table near some computer monitors. I was quickly flipping through the top images when I saw a photo of the safe house taken from an upper floor of a building nearby. Then there was a photo of a car taken from the same vantage point, showing Sarah in the passenger seat. I went on the headset and yelled, "The safe house is blown, send backup to location immediately!"

I grabbed my cellphone and called Sarah. "Is everything good there? Is your guard in the hallway?"

"I think so, why?"

"Move to the safe room right now, the door code is 2-0-4-0. I'm on my way. Don't open the door for anyone but me. This is just a precaution. I can't explain now. Just go."

Outside, something had alerted the guards, and I heard Carmichael say, "We've got company." As I came up the stairs, I could hear shots fired. Several armed vehicles were converging on the compound, and I could hear varied communications among drivers as to how to secure the area and close off the exits.

As I came to the storage unit door, I heard Carmichael say, "Two guards down, two more approaching from the back entrance to the main building."

I said, "I've got the guard on the left, you take the right." I knelt down and took aim, using my laser-equipped short-handled rifle. I went for the leg of the guard, hoping this would stop him from approaching any further. Carmichael had taken out the other guard. Two or three vehicles had come around the main building, and their headlights lit up the area. Agents exited the vehicles and approached the fallen guards, as a command was given: "Police officers! Stay down and place your hands behind you!"

I ran to the closest law-enforcement vehicle and yelled at the driver, "Turn this around! There's a problem at the safe house—that's where were going!"

"Yes sir," he responded.

It was about a ten-minute drive to the safe house, and I hoped there would be backup units already in route. "Sir, I've been informed there's been a front-entrance breach. Shots fired."

"There's an alley behind the property. We're going in through the back. Have you had combat training?" The driver shook his head. "Well, now you're going to get it."

We came down the alley, lights out, and parked a couple houses down from the property. "What gear do we have?"

"Sir, there's automatic rifles, concussion grenades, and smoke bombs in the back."

"Load up. Stay on my six and cover behind us." We could hear gunshots as we approached the back entrance. There was a coded entry lock, and no apparent entry had been made from here.

"K3, come in." K3 was the codename of the guard stationed outside Sarah's room. I repeated, "K3, are you there?" No reply. "What's your name?" I asked the driver.

"Agent Trevor Owens, sir."

"Okay Trevor. I'm going to the second floor. There's a staircase about twenty meters from here. Once I open this door, I'm going to throw a concussion grenade toward the stair entrance, then a smoke bomb. Use your thermal goggles to help see through the smoke. Stay low. Let's clear the kitchen and the front room first, then position yourself at the bottom of the stairs while I go up. You good?"

"Yes, sir."

I typed in the code and slowly opened the door a few inches. I could hear yelling in Russian inside the house. I rolled in the concussion grenade and pulled the door almost closed, and we both covered our ears. The impact from the explosion knocked us back a couple feet. I gathered myself and rolled in the smoke bomb. After a few seconds, we entered the kitchen, all clear, then proceeded to the front room. An armed assailant was lying on the floor, holding his ears and clearly disoriented. "Stay down!" I ordered. He reached for his weapon and I shot him in the head.

I could hear movement upstairs. As I slowly crept up the stairs, another gunman stepped out from the second floor landing. Before he could fire a shot, I sighted him with the laser scope and fired two shots, hitting him in the head and neck. Sarah's room was to the left. I reached the top of the stairs and threw another smoke bomb around the corner near the bedroom door. I let the hallway fill with smoke, then laid flat and inched out into the hallway, gun pointing toward the bedroom.

Immediately, shots flew over my head, and I returned fire with six shots. I could see the silhouette of a man fall to the ground just outside Sarah's room. I ran down the hallway, where I saw Agent K3 lying on the floor. The door to Sarah's room was slightly open, so I kneeled down and lightly tapped it about a foot further. A spray of bullets came through the door in response.

I lay down, reloaded my rifle, and inched into the opening. I emptied my clip around the room without catching a full view of what I hit, since I knew Sarah had gone to the safe room. I pulled back into the hallway, reloaded, and ran to a corner of the bedroom with a view to the safe room. There was one gunman lying on his side, holding his waist. In Russian I yelled out, "Don't move. Push your gun on the ground toward me." He complied and I walked to him. I pushed him onto his stomach and zip-tied his hands behind him.

The safe room door was closed. I banged on it and yelled out, "It's me, Sarah. René. I'm unlocking the door." I punched in the code and the door opened. Sarah was in the corner, shaking and crying. She slowly stepped away from the corner, recognized it was me, and ran to me. Still sobbing, we embraced and I told her,

"You're safe now, I got you, it's over." I pulled her head back from my chest and wiped away her tears, and we kissed.

We could hear sirens outside, along with the arrival of numerous vehicles. "All clear upstairs," I announced.

"Downstairs clear," I heard from Trevor.

We slowly left the safe room and the bedroom, and three agents ran up the stairs and met us at the door. "There's one inside," I said, pointing to the downed gunmen. We continued down the stairs and walked out the front door as more agents entered the house. With vehicle lights glaring

and megaphone announcements blasting for onlookers to clear the area, an agent escorted us to an unmarked vehicle.

As we drove away, I held Sarah closely. With her head on my shoulder, I kissed her hair and thanked god she was safe.

KEITH ALLAN
MISSION
REASSIGNED
IN HAVANA

Mission Reassigned in Havana

By

Keith Allan

Mission Reassigned in Havana

When they told me my first field assignment was going to be in Cuba, all I could envision was Gitmo and images of the Cuban Missile Crisis. I'd done my time at the farm, plus another year in the Cyber Division, learning information security and how to analyze decryption protocols. This was an offshoot of my studies at Princeton, but I made it clear I wanted to be out in the field, not stuck in a windowless dungeon full of computer nerds and reheated coffee. I received additional training in covert surveillance techniques and was lucky to be placed under the tutelage of a seasoned agent.

I arrived in Havana a few days ahead of schedule and was passing as a tourist on vacation. I soon had a very different view of life in Cuba, although Havana only provided a glimpse of what rural life in the countryside was like. I fell in love with the city. Amazing architecture, beautiful beaches, and the people were very friendly and always willing to help an American tourist obviously new to their enticing city. Havana is rich with an amazing blend of music, culture, and a nightlife that rivals the best in the world. Where else can you learn the hot salsa dance, sip on mojitos, and smoke the world-famous Cuban cigars? All of this was easily accessible by foot travel, passing through a maze of monuments, towering churches, and grand hotels. After two days, I almost forgot what I was there for, but my daily contact with a local agent kept me grounded in my purpose and mission objectives.

On the third day, I noticed a man I recognized from the day before, standing outside of my hotel. He looked like a Cuban national, dressed in a white suit, white fedora, and a floral print shirt. As I walked into town, I stopped at an outdoor café for an espresso and took a small table facing the street. My shadow had followed me there and was across the street, leaning against a lamppost, smoking a cigarette. I finished my coffee and continued my walk into town. I could see in an outside mirror of a car parked parallel to the curb that my tail had crossed the street and was now about thirty yards behind me. I turned right down a small alley and slipped into an inset doorway out of view. A minute later, he came down the alley as expected. I let him pass me, then I stepped behind him and grabbed his shirt behind his neck and pushed him against the alley's brick wall.

"I don't like being followed. Why are you following me?" I asked.

"I mean you no harm, señor. Please, no hurt me."

"Who sent you?"

"My boss, he only wants to talk with you. He's big business man. I give you his card, you call." With that, he started to reach inside his coat, so I jammed him further against the wall. "The card, just getting the card." He pulled out the card and held it over his shoulder. I grabbed the card but couldn't read it clearly in the alley.

"I'm here on vacation, and my wife will be joining me. If I see you again, you'll walk away with a limp or worse."

"Si, señor, si."

I pushed him toward the entrance of the alley. He stumbled a bit, then ran away in the direction he'd come from. I stepped back onto the sidewalk and read the card. It said *Blue Parrot Import and Export* and the name *Armando Joaquin.* It wasn't familiar, so it was hard to tell if he knew I was CIA, or if he wanted something else.

Just in case, I realized I might need a little insurance, so I called my contact and explained the situation. I'd have him run the name and company through the CIA database, and I also asked him to get me a handgun with a silencer. He said no problem, and we agreed to meet that afternoon at a museum close to the hotel. We met at the restroom there, where he handed me a late-model

Berretta and a few clips and said he should hear about the inquiry by morning.

On the fourth day, things began to take shape. I was to meet with a Russian national at a popular restaurant at noon. Her name was Maya Petracovich. Her official title was marketing consultant for a firm in St. Petersburg, Russia. This firm was a front for a Russian intelligence hub that worked primarily in the fields of data integrity and encryption techniques, and she was a data analyst. Her father was a big-time shipping entrepreneur who had recently passed away.

She had acquired new papers and a passport and was listed on the manifest of a luxury liner as a concierge. Her ship was due to arrive in Havana that morning. She had contacted the CIA with information regarding a string of recent computer hacks designed to cripple major waterways, and another data breach aimed at two major electricity hubs on the East Coast. She had requested asylum in the US in exchange for information regarding these incursions, and she could also provide decoding algorithms she had obtained while encrypting messages for the Russian government. I was to assess the validity of her information and, based on what I found, make a deal to provide her with a new identity and relocation in the US. We were to appear as husband and wife on vacation, and were to stay in Havana until the usefulness of her information could be determined.

I found a table in a somewhat isolated alcove at the restaurant. Close to noon, I saw Maya come into the restaurant, and as she looked around, I subtly waved to her. I had seen her picture in a bio, which didn't really do her justice. She was of medium height, had dark short-cropped hair, was slender in build, and had a rather nervous yet attractive gait. She acknowledged my wave and sat down across from me.

"Hello, I'm René," I said, and nodded.

She responded, "Maya, Maya Petracovich," while nodding in return.

"How was your trip?"

"It was okay, but a bit too long. It was my first cruise. I think I prefer flying."

"The food here is quite good, I understand; please have something to eat." I flagged down the waiter and he brought a couple of menus. "I believe you were briefed on the arrangement that was made, but let me explain a few details. We are to appear to be a married couple on vacation. I have a very nice hotel close by. My job is to evaluate the information you can provide and, based on what I find, either arrange a new identity and housing for you in the US, or, if for some reason the information has low value to our government, I can help you with travel arrangements to a foreign country of your choice. Is this your understanding of my government's communication with you?"

"Yes, it is. I will initially give you enough data to confirm the validity of what I have to offer you, and once this is vetted, I can complete the missing pieces in the data. Please understand, my father was a Russian patriot, but he was what I would call a centrist in the US—Soviet relationship. He disagreed with the recent Russian cyberattacks on US water and power facilities and believed in diplomacy over covert digital warfare. I'm fulfilling his wishes, and it is my wish that the US only use the information I can provide to stop, or at least slow down, these attacks—and not use it as an offensive tool."

"I can only forward the information to my superiors, with a provisional request relaying your wishes. It has been the policy of the US to take actions that do not directly affect the well-being of foreign citizens, but I am not a policy maker, I want that to be understood."

After a brief pause, I tilted my head. "May I ask where you learned to speak English so well? I read you graduated from Saint Petersburg State University, but your English is amazing."

"My mother was Dutch, and an English professor. My parents insisted that we spoke both English and Russian in the house. I studied information technology, but my second study was English literature."

"I'm so glad, because I have a very limited grasp of the Russian language." Smiling, I told her, "Please, order what you like."

After lunch, we strolled along the narrow streets. She seemed to light up with curiosity at people freely interacting, street musicians playing for tips, and the little children running and playing, so carefree.

As we were about to enter the hotel, I reminded her we were roleplaying as a married couple, which prompted her to grab my hand and look up at me with a warm smile. We proceeded to the fourth floor and entered our room. "I will be sleeping on the couch; your room is through here," and I opened the door ahead of her. She had a small suitcase which she laid on the bed.

"This is one of Havana's finest hotels, and the gift shop has a large selection of women's clothes. I see you packed light, so feel free to pick up anything you like downstairs. Here's some money to get you started; they accept American dollars. You'd probably like to freshen up, maybe shower, so I'll be in the front room when you're ready and we can go downstairs and visit the gift shop if you like."

"Thank you," she replied, and I closed the bedroom door behind me as I left her to it.

I could hear the shower running, and after about half an hour, she came out dressed in a modest flowing skirt, floral top, and slip-on white tennis shoes. "Do you approve?" and she did a twirl with a cute smile.

"You look lovely," which was a very honest response. "I have some new papers for you, a passport, and an extra room key. You will go by the name Nikita Sinclair, or just Nikki. We are from San Diego, California, where I work as a software engineer for a gaming company. It's important that we always go out together, never separately. I'm responsible for your safety, and since we're both new to Havana, we have to stay close and limit our conversations with others."

"I understand. When we get back to the room from shopping, I have a thumb drive with the initial data set for you to review. I take it you have access to a secure server?"

"Yes, it's through the American consulate. I can give it a preliminary review on my laptop, then pass it on to the folks at Langley. It may take a day or two to review, just so you know."

"That's fine. Can we go out into the city? This is such a beautiful place!"

"Sure, we need to keep up the married-couple-on-vacation appearance, and it is an amazing city. I've been here a couple days and love the people and the culture. Shall we go?" and I opened the door to the hallway.

Once we were at the gift shop, she fluttered around as if she were a teenager shopping for first-day-of-school clothes. She would occasionally ask my opinion on a dress or a blouse, holding it up to her chest. "What do you think? Too bright?" or "Too sexy?"

"Whatever you like—it all looks great."

We went back to the room and she hung up her new purchases. When she came out, she handed me a drive. "Here you go. There are a number of folders you can review. I believe there's enough there to confirm what I can offer you. If you have any questions, please let me know."

"Thanks." I inserted the thumb drive into my laptop and opened the first few folders. The markers that were there matched the signatures the CIA had discovered when analyzing the infrastructure hacks. There was additional coding that was like breadcrumbs that could lead to the source of the incursions. They were incomplete, as expected. I assumed they would be completed once a thorough review was made and an agreement with Maya was reached.

"This looks good so far. Let me pass it on." I sent the file to Langley via my secure network connection at the embassy.

"This room has a very secure safe where I store my laptop. I'm not sure where you keep your drives, but please keep them hidden. If you'd like to keep them in the safe, you're more than welcome. If you want to do that, the safe code is 23-17-6-41. You can open the safe and change the numbers. That way you can keep things safe, and even I will not have access; I can find another place for my laptop. It's up to you."

"I keep them on my person, in a very private place, but thank you," she said, smiling.

We left the hotel and strolled along the Malecón, a seaside boulevard on the north side of Old Havana. It was getting near sunset, so we stopped at a well-known restaurant and bar, El Floridita, one of Hemingway's favorites. The seafood was delicious, and we both indulged in a couple of mojitos. There was a Cabaret Tropicana show, followed by an amazing salsa band and dancing.

We decided to take a chance at dancing, and a local couple gave us some tips on dancing the rumba and mambo. She was a quick study, which made up for my two left feet. She guided me along, and though I wasn't in her league, I was at least in good company.

After a couple of hours, we took a cab back to the hotel. We were both a bit sauced, so once we were in our room, she grabbed me by the cheek and said, "So much fun, thank you!" and kissed me left and right in the European way. I closed the bedroom door and made myself comfortable on the couch.

In the morning, we went downstairs and had breakfast at the hotel's outdoor café. It was a beautiful morning, so she asked if we could lay out at the local beach. That sounded agreeable, so we went back to the room and changed into some swimwear. While she was in the bedroom, I got a call from my agency contact regarding the Blue Parrot inquiry. He mentioned that they were a legitimate import–export company with locations in Cuba, the Bahamas, and Jamaica. I wondered why, then, had I been followed, and what was the owner's business with me? I decided to call him later in the morning, just to see what his interest was.

She came out of her room in a black bikini, a sheer beach cover-up, a large floppy sun hat, and some oversized sunglasses. Once again I felt like she was out of my league, but maybe I would up my value by association.

The beach was part of the hotel property, private, with cabanas and an outdoor bar. We rented an umbrella and two beach chairs and found a nice spot in the sand. After about an hour, I asked her if she would like something to drink, and she said yes, some pineapple juice. I walked to the bar and ordered two juices.

While I was waiting, I decided to give Armando, the business owner, a call. After a few rings he picked up. "Hello?"

"My name is René Sinclair. I had a brief encounter with an associate of yours who was following me. He gave me your card and said I should call you."

"Yes, Señor Sinclair. Welcome to Havana! I'm sorry for the mix-up with Alejandro, he meant you no harm. I think we can be helpful to one another."

"How's that?" I asked.

"He first saw you at the American embassy and noticed they let you bypass security, very unusual. Are you a diplomat?"

"No, I help them with network security."

"You know the ambassador?"

"We've met, but only in regard to my work there."

"I would very much like to meet you. Would you come to my house for a visit? I can offer you the best drinks in all of Cuba, and a box of Cohiba cigars, the very best, not available to the public."

"I'm not sure what I can do for you. As I told Alejandro, I'm here on vacation and only stopped by the embassy to renew my passport."

"I have information about drug smuggling into the US that would be valuable to your country. I can have Alejandro drive you to my house; it's only about fifteen minutes from the city. Please, I love America and do a lot of business in your country."

"Let me get back to you."

I walked back to our spot on the beach and handed Maya her juice. We spent another hour at the beach, took a quick dip in the ocean, and strolled along the boardwalk. She bought some locally made jewelry, and we shared some fresh pineapple from a street vendor before we made our way back to the hotel. I needed to check in on the status of the information Maya had given me. She wanted a shower, so that would give me time to call in.

I got a secure line to Langley and mentioned my conversation with Armando. They said I should pursue the lead and see where it might go. They were still evaluating the data provided and said they should know whether it checks out by the morning.

If I was going to meet with Armando, I would need to know that Maya was safe, so I contacted the local CIA agent and arranged for him to come to the hotel and stay with her while I was gone. It was all set—Alejandro would pick me up at one thirty, and Javier, the local agent, would come up to our room at one fifteen.

Maya finished her shower and changed. When she came out, I told her I had some company business to take care of, and Javier would be staying with her. I promised I'd be gone no more than two hours, after which we could go out for dinner and catch some entertainment. She seemed okay with this but was a little reluctant to be in the company of a stranger. I assured her he was a trained agent, and I would be no more than two hours.

Javier arrived at one ten. I introduced the two and went downstairs. At about one thirty-five, I saw Alejandro pull up in a dusty open-air jeep. I climbed in. "Hello Señor Sinclair, we be there shortly."

We headed out of town, took a couple exits off the main road, and drove along a dirt road. The terrain was desertlike—flat and sandy, with the occasional shrub decorating the rather barren landscape. We came to a stop at a sort of checkpoint. There was a guard in old desert fatigues, sitting under a makeshift sunblock made of two-by-fours and palm fronds. The compound was fenced in with barbed wire. There was a rotating video camera mounted on a tall pole next to the gate entrance. The guard got out of his chair and pushed open the gate. Alejandro gave him a little wave, and we drove through.

About a hundred yards ahead was a large old rundown-but-elegant house. We walked up some stairs to the veranda, passing a pair of white pillars leading to the front door. The doors opened ahead of us, and a man looking to be about fifty years old, with gray hair and a beard, greeted us.

"Hello, hello, come in, come in! I'm Armando Joaquin. I'm so glad you decided to come." He extended his hand, and as I was shaking it, I said, "René Sinclair."

The house was cluttered with artwork, paintings stacked next to each other, a number of sculptures, and a variety of what appeared to be locally made weavings, picture frames, and a few rugs—some rolled up and some laid out. "Excuse the mess, some of the local artists drop off their work unannounced, so everything's kind of unorganized right now. Come, come, let's got to my study." A maid came out of another room, and Armando yelled out, "Two cognacs, bring the Louis XIII."

We entered the study, which was equally cluttered, with books lying about, a rather impressive library, and a large antique desk, which he sat behind. Sunlight streamed through two windows in an otherwise unlit room. You could see specks of dust floating in the light, and the musky fragrance of old leather and cigar smoke added to the ambiance.

Framed photos of Che Guevara and Castro were on the wall across from me, and another of Batista with his arm over the shoulder of another gentleman. Armando noticed my gaze and said, "I am a merchant, like my father, and his father. My grandfather fought with Guevara and the rebel army against Batista but later distanced himself from the movement. He supported the rising artists that evolved in the late '50s and '60s and began a small exporting business in Mexico, and a few years later in Cuba. I am not political; I don't concern myself with such things. I only deal with politics when it involves my business concerns. I'm not a communist or a socialist, I'm merely a merchant trying to support the arts."

The maid entered the study and set a tray with the cognacs on the desk. "Please, the cognac is quite lovely," and Armando motioned at the tray.

I reached for a glass and took a small sip. "Excellent," I replied.

"You must also try one of Cuba's finest cigars. You will find no better in the world." He opened a cigar box on the desk, spun it around, and slid it in my direction. Though it was a bit early in the day to drink or smoke, it was only polite to accept his hospitality. I reached for a cigar, and as I did, he handed me a cigar cutter and a lighter. After a few minutes of indulging in what was truly an exceptional smoke, I leaned back in my chair and redirected the conversation.

"I appreciate the kind invitation to your house. What information do you have that can be helpful to the US, and what is it you would like in return?"

"In my business, I meet many people in shipping. One such person has contacted me a number of times about moving his product in one of my shipping containers that makes port in Miami. I have declined his request, though I keep an open, somewhat friendly relationship with him. This is because he is a very powerful and dangerous man, and to dismiss him outright would be unwise.

"This man also has a luxury yacht company, under a different name, in Miami. He takes celebrity couples and fashion models and photographers on weekend trips from Miami to Bimini. One of my close business friends has a slip next to his in Bimini. My friend has security cameras that rotate around his property and he has seen people late at night loading duffle bags into the lower deck of the luxury yachts. Potentially hundreds of pounds of cocaine could be loaded in the cargo holds of the yachts."

"What is it you would like out of this?"

"For years, I have tried to establish an import business in Miami. I've submitted all the required documents, business permits, and other legal forms. Every year they refuse, citing a limited number of permits available and some difficulty with trade agreements with Cuba. In exchange for my information, I would like to be granted a business license and assurances from the US that all necessary permits and agreements to conduct such a business will be granted."

This was a very complicated request, and I certainly didn't have the authority to grant it. It did, however, seem in the scope of possibility. "I'm not in a position to make such an agreement, but I can take it to my superiors for their consideration. For now, I will keep our conversation just between you and me. There is a person at the consulate I can speak to that can determine what all would need to take place, and if this is even possible. Can you give me a couple days?"

"Of course, I understand. Please let me know what you find out. You can reach me anytime by calling the number on the card.

For now, enjoy your drink and cigar, and Alejandro can drive you back to town whenever you are ready."

On the way back to the hotel, I tried to envision how this all could be done. My primary objective was of course validating the data that Maya had brought, and providing safe passage for her to the US, should things check out.

I arrived at the hotel and made my way upstairs to the room. Maya appeared to be glad to see me, and she gave me a little hug. I thanked Javier, and he left the room. It was getting late in the afternoon, so I suggested to Maya that we take a cab to a well-known restaurant on the outskirts of town. She was excited to see more of the city, and she went inside her room to change.

I used this time to call Langley and relay the proposition Armando had presented me. They said that if we were to pursue this, it would need to involve the DEA in Miami, and possibly Interpol in Bimini. I suggested that a female agent and I could pose as a couple recently engaged, or possibly on our honeymoon, and arrange to take the weekend boat trip from Miami to Bimini. This would give me the opportunity to survey the boat landing in Bimini and give relevant intelligence to the authorities, whether that's Interpol or whatever agency would be involved on that end. The supervisor at Langley said he would initiate a multi-agency task force and get back to me soon.

Maya came out of her room in a stunning black dress with a white belt. It was cut just above the knee, form fitting, with small straps over her shoulders. She wore black heels and a large floppy hat with a black crown and white brim. She was quite stunning, and I quickly realized I needed to change into something more elegant. I had brought a black blazer and trousers, so I coupled it with a black silk shirt and a white tie.

Our cab driver drove a '60s Cadillac and acted as a tour guide as we passed through the city, pointing out various landmarks. It reminded me of one of those Hollywood tour buses, where they drive through the hills pointing out where certain celebrities live.

The restaurant had a large dance floor and a performance stage. There were tables surrounding the dance floor and a few tables on the second floor that overlooked the main room. I requested one of those tables, and after a twenty-dollar tip to the maître d', we were escorted upstairs. The room was thick with smoke and filled with a blend of aromas, including spicy Latin foods, perfumes, and cedar wood from the building's structure.

I was dying for a good steak, and I had heard this was the place to get it. I've always been found of rum drinks, so I ordered us a pair of mai tais. Maya was proving not only to be very intelligent but to have a kind of sophistication you see in women of means from Russia and other Eastern European countries.

We talked about her past and growing up in St. Petersburg. She was a ballet student from the age of six and was being groomed for a place in the Bolshoi Ballet Company. At the age of thirteen, her interest shifted to the theater, and her father enrolled her in acting classes, hoping she would perform on the stage. She confessed that her real desire was to work in films and eventually travel to the West to work with her favorite directors. Upon receiving a scholarship to study mathematics and digital technology, however, she postponed her acting career, partly due to her need to be near her father and provide him with comfort and the care he needed to battle his many health issues.

After a glorious meal and another chance to redeem my marginal dancing skills, we hailed a cab and returned to the hotel. At this point, it was becoming as much a relationship as it was an assignment. The temptation to advance the relationship to a physical one was a real test of my professional oath. She was a woman of sophistication, and I must confess I had never met anyone like her. Now I knew how Adam felt when he saw Eve, and I've always loved apples.

As we entered the hotel room, my higher plans of separating work and pleasure fell aside. She pulled me to her and kissed me. We were both quite vulnerable at this point, and though she had no company rules to follow, I returned her embrace as if mine never existed. She pulled back slightly, just enough to start removing my jacket, and then the clasp of my belt. I lowered the straps on her dress and they fell down her arms. This caused the front of her dress to fall to her waist, revealing her breasts. I kissed her neck, and as I did, she put her thumbs in the sides of her dress at the waist, and it dropped to the floor. I wrapped my arms around her, lifted her up, and she encircled my waist with her legs. I stepped back out of my fallen pants and carried her to the bedroom. I laid her back on the bed and started kissing her breasts and stomach, eventually ending up between her legs. She put her hands behind my head, guiding me where she wanted me, and arched her back up and down. She was the most passionate woman I had ever experienced, and we made love late into the night.

In the morning, I woke before she did, and I ordered coffee, espresso, and croissants from room service. The bed was a mess, and I pulled back the drapes to let the morning light warm her naked figure. At that moment, I wished I were a painter, and I suddenly understood the inspiration that came to the world's most talented artists. I sat in a chair and couldn't help but stare at the wonder before me.

The doorbell rang, so I reluctantly got up to answer it. I took the tray from the server's hands, handed him a few dollars, and quietly shut the door behind him. Maya was stirring in the bed as I approached her. She sat up and pulled the white sheet up to her waist. One of the things about European women that makes them so naturally appealing is their comfort with nudity. It's a cultural attribute that removes shame and any form of embarrassment from viewing the nude form and allows God's most astonishing form of beauty to awaken to the eye of the beholder.

"Good morning," I said.

"Would you set the tray on the end table?"

As I set the tray down, she grabbed my arm and pulled me onto her. We kissed for what seemed like a lifetime, and when we finally pulled back a few inches, she said "Yes it is!"

Needless to say, by the time we got around to the espresso, it was quite cold.

We both needed showers, so I finally got up from the bed and walked toward the door, glancing behind me to see her skipping to the bathroom. There is a point in life where you no longer fear death, because you have seen or experienced something unforgettable and life altering. This may sound like a person experiencing an epiphany, because it was.

I called in to see the status on Maya's data analysis and if a decision had been made on the Miami drug case. They said Maya's info looked pretty solid, and they were in the process of establishing a location for her move to the states and creating a new identity for her.

They also wanted to move on the proposal that Armando had to offer. They were only willing to grant him a business license and the necessary permits for a business in Miami if a bust was made in Miami with tangible results, meaning a drug seizure of the scale he had indicated. Also, they wanted to track down the source in Bimini, and hopefully determine how the drugs got to Bimini, to lead to a larger scale of arrest warrants on that end.

I would need to connect with Armando and explain how things would need to proceed, and see if he was agreeable to the terms. I called him and told him things looked good, but we would need to meet so I could explain the conditions. He said he was driving in to Havana that afternoon and offered to take me to lunch. I told him that would be fine, and I would be bringing my wife if that was okay. He said, "Yes, please do, I'm sure she's a wonderful woman."

After I had showered, Maya and I sat in the front room to plan our day. "I have some good news. My agency is ready to go forward with your agreement, and they are securing a new location and identity for you back in the states."

"Oh, that's wonderful!" she said excitedly. "Can I live in California or Florida? That's always been a dream of mine."

"I can see if that's possible, but I can't guarantee it; those are rather high-profile states, and I know they will want to make your safety the number-one priority.

"Today, we'll be having lunch with a local businessman, so we need to make sure we have our histories rehearsed in case he asks us any questions about our pasts. Of course, we can't let him know anything about your reason for coming to Havana or about my agency.

"I'm working on another case that this gentleman, his name is Armando, will be helping me with. Some of what we need to discuss is somewhat private, so I'm going to arrange for Javier, the guy that stayed with you yesterday, to come to our table at the restaurant, posing as a waiter, and say there is a call for you in the restaurant lobby. We can say it's a college friend of yours we are meeting up with later to lay out at the beach. If you could give us about ten minutes, that should be enough time for us to discuss what we need to. Is that okay?"

"Of course, that will be easy," she said. We spent the next half hour inventing a plausible history of our relationship.

We arrived at the restaurant, and the maître d' greeted us as if he was expecting us. "Mister René? I have your table ready, it's Armando's favorite." He escorted us to the table, and Armando got out of his chair for the introduction.

"This is Nikki. Nikki, Armando."

"I'm honored. I hope you're enjoying your time in Havana." With that, he took her outstretched hand and gently kissed the back of it.

"It's a beautiful country, so full of culture and history," she replied.

We sat down, and the waiter brought us the menus and water. "Champagne for my friends, and a sample of your finest hors d'oeuvres." We exchanged some chitchat and ordered food. Shortly after we ordered, Javier came to the table. "There's a call for Miss Nikki in the lobby. From your friend Alexa?"

"Oh, thank you. I'll be right back." I explained to Armando about the beach plans the two were making.

"I've heard from my government, and they are willing to agree to your request, but under the condition that an arrest for smuggling drugs be made in Miami before we can grant you the necessary paperwork required for a business in Miami. This is not negotiable. If you agree to this, we can sign an affidavit stating the terms of our arrangement."

"That is fine with me. I don't like people that traffic in drugs, and if I can help stop this, I would feel good that I made a contribution to this cause."

"Great. The US government has made halting the import of illegal drugs a top priority, and your assistance would be much appreciated. What I would need from you is the name of the individual that contacted you, and the name of the luxury yacht company that operates out of Miami. Let's plan on meeting tomorrow at the US consulate, and I will have the affidavit drawn up and ready for you. If you require your attorney to be present, please let me know their name so I can inform the consulate."

"I don't think that will be necessary. I trust you and the US to stand by your word."

"Sounds good. Say, noon tomorrow?"

"Perfect."

Maya came back from the lobby, and we rose from our chairs and sat down. "Everything set with Alexa?" I asked.

"Yes! We are meeting at three thirty."

After lunch, we said goodbye to Armando and hailed a cab. We returned to the hotel. "Would you like to go to the beach for a couple hours?"

"I would, it's so gorgeous out today."

While she was changing for the beach, I called in to get any updates on the operations. I was forwarded to the task-force leader in charge of the Miami operation.

"Here's how we see this happening. We are going to have you flown to Miami, and you'll register for a weekend trip to Bimini.

You will have a female agent accompany you, as you suggested. Once you arrive in Bimini, we will need you to survey the docking point and place a tiny video camera with a clear view of the yacht. We must gather sufficient visual evidence that a smuggling group is using the yacht to transport drugs or some other contraband, in order to get the approval of the Bahamian authorities to proceed. We will have you and the female agent continue with your weekend agenda and not alert any of the staff associated with the trip about your mission. It must appear exactly as what you signed up for—a weekend holiday to the Bahamas.

"After you've obtained more details, we will have Interpol agents readied, and they will handle the operation from there. Once you return to Miami and you have disembarked, we will close in and secure the yacht with the assistance of the DEA. When will you know the yacht company's name, and the name of the kingpin?"

"I'm meeting with Armando at noon tomorrow. He has agreed to the terms we discussed."

"Good. We believe we already know the yacht company operating out of Miami; there are only a few that fit the description you've given us. Here's my direct number—call me after your meeting with Armando. We need to move quickly on this."

"Yes sir, will do."

Maya had changed, so I put on some shorts and grabbed a shirt. We headed down to the beach and again rented a couple of chairs and an umbrella. I ordered two mojitos, and we settled into a quiet spot on the sand. I decided to bring her up to speed on her deal with Langley. "Things are looking good with the data you gave us. In a couple days they will let me know what, if any, options you have for a place to live in the US. I told them you'd like to be in

Florida or California, so hopefully they can accommodate you. I have another assignment in Miami in a few days, so I may not be able to accompany you when you travel to your new home."

"Oh, Miami? What will you be doing there?"

"I can't really discuss any details, but I'll be going on a short cruise to the Bahamas, just to make some observations."

"Can I come? We could go as a couple, like we are now. We know each other very well," she said, with a mischievous smile, "and I won't be in the way."

"I don't think my superiors would approve. They would be concerned with your safety . . . as would I.".

"Okay, tell them I insist on going. If they agree, I will give you the final data set today. They can authenticate it, and if it proves to be useful, I go to Miami."

I was in a tight spot. The CIA likes to call the shots and doesn't like outside interference. On the other hand, if her new data provides them with what they are looking for, they might be more agreeable to her idea. Also, we have had time to develop a relationship as a couple, so it would be easy enough to pull off our ruse again. "I can run it by my superior and see what he says. I can't guarantee it'll happen; we'll just have to see."

"Yay! When they see what's on my second drive, they will be amazed. They wouldn't be able to find out the sources of the cyberattacks against your country in any other way."

After a night of room service and a fine bottle of single-malt scotch, we found it quite easy to sleep in late. I told Maya I needed to meet with Armando at the consulate at noon. Javier would stay with her at the hotel. I had told Armando to enter the consulate via a private entrance in the back of the building. This would keep his presence at the consulate more secure.

He arrived on time, and we were escorted to Javier's empty office to hear what Armando had to say. He was presented with the affidavit we had discussed, which he read through briefly and signed. "The person that you are interested in is Joaquin Espinosa. He is the head of the Hermanos de Sangre cartel. He operates out of Cartagena, Colombia. The yacht company in Miami is called Dreamline Cruises. It is registered under the name Richard Keating, a local entrepreneur that fronts Espinosa's business interests in Miami.

"Espinosa is a man without a conscience. He is responsible for dozens of murders in Colombia and has eluded capture for many years, partly due to his alliance with the police and his generous support of the Colombian army. Please do not associate me with any aspect of your proceedings. I will remain on friendly terms with him, should he continue to contact me."

"We are quite familiar with the Sangre cartel. I can assure you the information you have provided will never find its way back to you. Thank you for your cooperation; we'll get back to you soon. The guard in the hallway will show you the way out of the building."

After he left the office, I called Langley and relayed the information Armando had provided. I also told them what Maya had proposed. "Hold the line, please." There was a pause in the conversation, and I could faintly hear some discussion taking place among a group of people. Back on the line, "If her new data pans out, do you think she is capable of doing this? She must know that we could not guarantee her safety, and that any connection between her and the agency would be denied emphatically."

"I think we could pull it off. We have spent a few days together and have established a comfortable relationship. If I were to be paired with a female agent, it would be difficult to pull off with the same level of familiarity as I have with Maya. Whatever you think. I'll be at this office for the next hour or so if you've made a decision by then."

"I'll let you know soon," he replied.

I used Javier's computer to check out Dreamline Cruises. Reservations must be made at least two days in advance for the Bimini weekend cruises. They leave on a Friday at noon, arrive in Bimini at about two, then return at two on that Sunday. I looked at their online booking calendar and there was an opening for one couple that week. It was Tuesday, so if we got the green light to proceed, we might be able to secure our spot. They showed the itinerary for the trip, and the guest accommodations were in the house where the yacht was docked. The photos gave a pretty clear picture of the property. The itinerary was well defined, with a footnote that all guests must stay with the group, and a guide to various destinations on the island would be provided.

After about an hour, I got a return call from Langley. They gave the okay on using Maya as my partner on the Florida operation. I left the building and returned to the hotel. I told Maya that my superior had approved using her as my wife in the Miami. They wanted to get the second set of data as soon as possible. She went in her room, came out, and handed me another flash drive.

"Let me get this off to Langley," I said. "They will be very pleased to see it." I went to my laptop and sent the files. While I was there, I went online and booked the remaining seats at Dreamline Cruises. They would be leaving on Friday at noon. It was Tuesday, so I booked a flight out of Havana for Wednesday.

Maya was very excited for the Bimini trip, and she had always wanted to go to Miami. I reminded her that we were going as a married couple, and it was very important that we keep the roles we had already established for the entire trip, both in Miami and during the Bimini trip.

"I enjoy being your pretend wife," she said, smiling. "This is like a dream vacation for me. I've never been out of Russia, and I'm sure my father is looking down at me with pride at carrying out his desire to keep our two great powers in balance."

"Our country appreciates what you are doing, and personally, being here with you has been wonderful. You are quite a woman."

With that, she came over to me and put her arms around me, and we kissed. My immediate thoughts were to make her safety my number-one priority, even above my country. I would not be willing to sacrifice her life to catch a drug lord. Not a chance.

On Wednesday, we arrived in Miami and checked into a hotel. A little more bikini shopping was in order, and we split our time between the hotel pool and the beach. The folks at Langley gave me a list of restaurants I could choose from, and they would have us shadowed while we were there.

On Friday, we checked in at Dreamline, signed some disclosures, and turned in our luggage. The yacht was a forty-five-foot outboard beauty, and as we waited to board, we exchanged some casual conversation with a few of the other passengers. A celebrity couple, a model–photographer team, and some other rather wealthy-looking couples that obviously wanted to keep to themselves. It took a little over two hours to get to Bimini, and Maya found a place on the deck to work on her tan.

The yacht pulled up parallel to the dock, and we were escorted onto a walkway running down the shoreline. Our guide took us to our residence, which was directly across from where the yacht was docked. There were a few steps up to a pool area and a large deck littered with lounge chairs, tables, and an outdoor bar. The house, more like a mini resort, was divided into two parts: one for the guests and one for the workers. We were shown our room, which was beautifully furnished but had no windows facing the dock.

My job was to place video cameras overlooking the yacht and front deck area, and also on the opposite side of the residence facing the street. I was told that the street side was already under surveillance, with the goal of tracking the source of incoming traffic back to where the drugs were stored, and hopefully running down how they got to the island. The cameras were extremely small, about the size of a dime. The trick was placing them when no one was around.

I had given the entry area a good look as we were shown off the yacht, and I'd found a couple of locations that would work. There were security cameras mounted on the eaves of the overhang covering the sun deck. I'd have to avoid those when placing my cameras. Mine had peel-off sticky backs, and their images were sent via Wi-Fi to the surveillance team nearby. According to the itinerary, Friday night we would be driven into town to an upscale restaurant, and Saturday there would be a barbeque outdoors at the residence. It would be best to place the cameras at night, so the plan was to venture out onto the deck when we returned from dinner the first night. Hopefully there wouldn't be any relevant activity while we were away.

Just in case, I decided to see if I could get one camera placed before dinner. I told Maya what I was up to and that it might be useful to have her join me in case I needed a distraction. She was up for it and liked the idea of playing a part in the scheme. Dinner was scheduled for seven, so about six thirty we left our room and headed to the outside deck. It was hot and humid, that kind of tropical feel where you're sticky with sweat all the time. Maya dressed in a black one-piece bathing suit with a sheer black cover-up. This in itself was a distraction.

As we walked out onto the open deck, I noticed one other couple grabbing the last few minutes of sunlight. I let Maya walk ahead of me and told her to get their attention. She strolled over to a lounge chair near the couple, and "accidentally" spilled her drink. The man and woman both sat up, ready to help. Between her attire and the spillage, I had plenty of time to stick a camera on a waist-high trash can located on the side of the deck. I hurried down to join Maya, and I thanked the couple. "Let me get you some more wine."

She walked back with me to the bar, and we ordered the wine. We rejoined the couple, introduced ourselves, and took a couple lounge chairs next to them. After a few minutes, the four of us got up and went to the front of the residence, where a tour-bus type of vehicle was waiting.

After dinner we returned to the house, and Maya and I went to our room to regroup. I needed to place one or two more cameras with a clear view of the yacht, so I told Maya we should go out on the deck and have a drink. They had a strict curfew at midnight, with no access to the outside of the house. Their reason was for the safety of the guests, citing an incident with a tourist that took place a couple of months ago.

When we got to the deck, there were two other couples at the bar. I suggested to Maya that we go for a stroll down the walkway running along the dock. Things were fairly quiet on our walk, just an occasional passerby and not much activity. As we approached our place, there was a bench one house down from us. I mentioned to Maya we should sit for a short while, and this gave me time to stick another camera with a clear view of the yacht. After a few minutes, we walked back to the deck area and found a couple of chairs next to a couple we sat next to at dinner.

At one point, I excused myself and went inside the house. There was a mosaic artwork off to the side of the glass doorway leading inside the house, and it was filled with round glass pieces that resembled one of my cameras. I chipped off one of the pieces and replaced it with a camera. My apologies to the artist. I walked back to the chairs with fresh glasses of wine for Maya and me. After some brief storytelling by the other couple, Maya and I excused ourselves and headed for our room. Once there, I got a secure message from the surveillance team that all three cameras were functioning well. They also informed me there was no need for additional cameras in the front of the property—they had it covered.

On Saturday, the group was taken to the far side of the island, where an old shipwreck lay scattered along the shoreline. It was definitely a photo-op addition to the itinerary, along with sunbathing and swimming in the crystal-clear water. Our host brought along a picnic-like lunch, as well as some rum and a variety of mixers the guests could choose from. Maya was loving it all, and I must admit, this was my kind of assignment.

In the afternoon, they drove us to an open-air market, where vendors were selling everything from fruits and vegetables to local artwork. There was even a calypso band playing in the middle of the square, with locals and tourists listening and dancing. We picked up some local-made blouses and a handwoven bracelet, and put away a few Red Stripes. When we came back to the house, they were barbecuing steaks and mahi-mahi, per everyone's order taken in the morning. They had brought out a large banquet table to accommodate the whole group, and the food was excellent. After dinner, a flamenco guitarist played a variety of Latin-based songs, and a few of the guests showed their intolerance for alcohol. About eleven o'clock, things were wrapped up, so we went back to our room.

The next morning, I received a message from the surveillance team that they got what we needed to secure a search warrant back in Miami. They also had followed a van, which had delivered the product, back to a warehouse, and the plan was to raid the warehouse at the same time as the Miami search, so no one would be tipped off from either location. At this point, my job was done. We would just enjoy the rest of our trip and hope everything culminated in arrests made on both ends.

Sunday's plans started out with a continental breakfast, followed by a trip to some sand dunes on the opposite side of the island from the shipwreck, and some ATV rentals. This was very cool, and Maya and I got a caged dune buggy and took off across the dunes. I had done this one other time in Pismo Beach, and Maya was beside herself, laughing hysterically as she gripped the hand supports to keep from banging against the inside of the cage.

After a couple of hours, we went back to the house and packed our luggage for a three o'clock departure. We boarded the yacht and took off for Miami. There was some afternoon wind chop on the water, which made for a bumpy ride back. As Miami came into view, I pulled Maya aside, stressed the importance of keeping our disguise in play, and told her the raid would take place within minutes of our arrival. She seemed to take it all in stride, but I knew these things could often get out of hand, and there were always risks involved.

The dock had a large open area adjacent to it, with spaces for parking, drop offs, and cab service. There was a building, a short distance from where we docked, where passengers showed their ID and passports. The raid would have to be timed after everyone had been processed and were out of harm's way. I had noticed a large van in the lot, and a number of other vehicles. It was difficult to tell how things would go down, but the agency had enough time to survey the area and put together a plan.

We were the last couple to be checked in at the processing building, and as we were about to leave the room, I heard a loud conversation in Russian coming from the room next door. I looked out toward the docking area and saw DEA agents running toward the yacht. There was a door connecting our room to the room where I heard the shouting. The person that checked us in appeared to be in shock, looking at us, at the happenings outside, and at the connecting door. I pushed Maya behind me and situated us in such a way that, should the connecting door swing open, we would be behind it. The door flew open, and two men ran for the door we'd come in through. By this time, agents had surrounded the building, and the two men were quickly apprehended.

Out on the dock, the yacht had started up and was attempting to get away. The two crew members on the boat fired automatic rifles at the DEA agents, who quickly returned fire. One of the crew dropped and the other set down his gun and held up his hands. The harbor police blocked the yacht's escape, and the captain shut down his motors. We stepped out the door, exiting the building with our hands up. I had my agency badge in my left hand, and I identified myself to the agents. Maya was noticeably shaken, so I put my arm around her shoulders and said, "It's over, it's over, we're good now."

A CIA agent approached me. "René, come with me. We'll need to debrief you at the Miami station; it shouldn't take too long."

At the station, we were greeted by the task-force leader and ushered to his office. "We should hear back from the Bimini team soon, but things are looking good." He asked me and Maya a series of questions, piecing together the timeline of events and verifying the information we had provided. After about half an hour, his phone rang. I could tell he was getting an update on the operation. He hung up and filled us in.

"Okay, here's the status. They raided the warehouse in Bimini and confiscated several dozen kilos of cocaine and a number of weapons. They made several arrests at the warehouse and the residence. They're questioning a number of those that were arrested, and it looks like we'll get some good intel on how the drugs got to the island. Also, inside the cargo holds of the yacht we found sixty more kilos of cocaine. Good work, you two. We've wanted to get this guy for a long time. At the very least, we've cut off a supply chain of his and ruffled his feathers.

"Just to be safe, we're moving you two to a different hotel. I think you'll like it. Oh, and Maya, the data you provided checked out. Your relocation arrangements are being finalized. We couldn't do Florida, but I think you'll like Southern California—a little beach town called Carlsbad. We're through here; you two can pack and an agent will drive you to your new hotel. Your station chief offered to give you two a couple more days to relax before you fly to California. Sound good?"

"Yay! I'm so happy!" Maya shouted.

We packed up our things and were driven to the new hotel. When we got to our room, I turned to Maya and said, "What do you think?"

She rushed to my arms and we kissed. She finally pulled back a few inches and said, "I love America, and it's because of you!" For a first assignment, this was amazing; but even more amazing was the woman that made it possible.

KEITH ALLAN
MESSAGE LEFT
UNHEARD

Message Left Unheard

By

Keith Allan

Message Left Unheard

Knock, knock, knock.

Damn it! So much for a clean escape. Ten till five and some idiot can't wait a day. As I walk to the door, Theodore, the cat, follows at my feet. "Can I help you?" I ask, as I crack the door just a few inches to keep Theo from running away again.

On the other side is an attractive fortysomething woman who looks vaguely familiar. "Mr. Pierson?" she asks.

"No, he's out of town on a case. Check back early next week."

"Can you help me? I think my daughter's in trouble," she says, as she inches closer, making her cleavage known.

That's Theo's cue, and he slips between my legs and ventures out into the hallway. "Oh, I'll get him," the visitor says. He would run from me, see it as a game of chase, but for her he just stops, looks up at her, and meows. Traitor. She picks him up and he nestles snugly into her rather significant bosom.

So, of course, they come inside, and my early exit plan implodes. "Have a seat," I offer. "I should tell you I'm really just an assistant, not a PI. I just do a little surveillance and identity tracking on the computer," hoping this would discourage her from any further discussion.

"My daughter and I text every afternoon, and she hasn't responded for two days. A friend recommended your agency, and I don't know where else to turn."

I've got to come up with more intimidating exit lines, like "sorry, we're closed," and shut the door. "Your daughter, does she live in the area?" I ask.

"She's a senior at USC and lives with three roommates in a rented house in Venice. Here's her name, address, and phone number," and she hands me a slip of paper.

Aha; I thought I recognized mom's face. Gloria Van Holtz, and her daughter is Regina. The Van Holtzes own half the valley, and Gloria's a well-known socialite in the LA area.

"Here's a retainer to get you started, and here's my number. Please call as soon as you find out anything. My daughter and I haven't been getting along lately, and I feel like maybe it is something I did or said." She hands me an envelope stuffed with cash, and her business card. She never even asked about a fee structure, but I guess money isn't a great concern.

"I can do a little looking, but I'm a law student and don't have a license as a private investigator," I tell her.

"You look like a capable young man; I have faith in you," and she sets down Theo and makes her way toward the door. When she leaves, I look inside the envelope. It's stuffed full of hundreds, and I'm feeling like a drug deal just went down; no paper trail, no contract, just an intern with a bunch of Franklins and a cat that is yacking for his dinner. This should be fun . . . or maybe a disaster.

The Venice boardwalk is kind of an outdoor version of that famous bar scene in a Star Wars movie. There's the Muscle Beach guys pumping iron and dripping sweat, a Rollerblade pair of guys in Speedos putting the gay in gay, and an assortment of hippy chicks that missed the sixties so they're putting a new spin on it. I locate the street I'm looking for, about a half a block in from the sand. There's no street numbers visible on the houses I've narrowed it down to, so I see a group of kids nearby, practicing kick-flips on their skateboards.

"Do you know which house is 2654?" I ask them.

"Who are you looking for?" one of them asks.

"Regina?" I respond.

"Gina? Yeah, over there," and points me in the right direction.

The leader of the pack speaks up: "Sure could use a Coke!"

"Sure, here you go" and I hand them each a single.

"Thanks, dude," I get back.

The house is a two-story amazement, black with gold trim, with a variety of wind chimes and dangly things hanging from the porch. "My dad said it was a brothel like a hundred years ago, whatever that is," a skater boy reveals.

I climb the steps leading up to the front door. A few knocks and a few moments later, the door opens. A girl about Gina's age answers, wearing only a bra and underwear. Looks like someone forgot to take off their makeup before bed, and her hair would make Einstein proud. "Yeah?" leaks from her mouth, with some effort required.

"I'm looking for Gina. Is she here?" I ask.

"She hasn't been home for a couple nights. Who are you?"

"I work for a private investigator. Do you know where she might be? A boyfriend, maybe?"

"Not sure. She works at the Alamo doing bottle service, you might try there," she informs me.

"Okay, thanks. Here's my card, and my number's on the back. Could you have her call me if she gets back?"

"So you're a private investigator?" she asks.

"No, I'm just a law student and work part-time for this agency."

"Ew, a someday lawyer, even better! You can investigate my privates anytime."

That was a bit unexpected and embarrassing. I chuckled and turned to make an exit.

"I'm Wendy, by the way," she yells out.

"Thanks Wendy, see you later."

"You certainly can," she replies, and teasingly lowers her bra strap.

The Alamo is a high-scale club in Hollywood, just off the strip. I've been there a couple of times and know one of the bouncers. That evening, I called my boss to let him know what was going on, but I had to leave a voicemail. I arrived at the club around

10:00 p.m., and Tim was working the front door. "Hey, what's up?" he asks.

"Not much. Do you know a girl named Gina that works here?"

"Yeah, she's sweet. Not on tonight. Talk to Mike at the bar, he kind of knows what everyone's up to."

"Thanks, man," and he lets me in. It's loud and crowded, very typical for this place. There are a couple of bartenders; so I make a guess which one might be Mike. "Just a Heineken. Are you Mike?"

"Yep, what can I do for you?" as he pops the top of my beer.

"I'm trying to find Gina. Have you seen her lately?" I ask him.

"Two nights ago, she was working. Got off around two. Why?"

"She hasn't been home since then. Just trying to find her and make sure she's okay. If you hear from her, could you tell Tim? He's a friend and knows how to get ahold of me."

"Sure thing. Hey, she parks down the street, a gray BMW, if that helps."

"Thanks, appreciate it," I respond. I leave the club and go look for her car. A couple hundred yards down, I spot it. It's locked, and there's no sign it's been messed with.

As I'm walking around it, a guy across the street yells out, "Looking for someone?"

"Yeah, the girl that owns this car," I yell back.

"A couple nights ago I saw a van pull up, and I think she got inside. I couldn't see too much from here, but that van flew out of here in a hurry."

This sounded bad. I walked over to his side of the street. "Can you describe the van?"

"Yeah, it was a blue Caravan. Couldn't tell you the year, but I think the first three letters on the plate was JLM, if that helps."

"Great, sure does. Thanks a lot!" This sounded like a kidnapping, but there wasn't enough to go on to bring the police into it yet. Besides, they would just ask a few questions, and it was doubtful they would assign a detective to the case at this point.

I had two approaches I could follow next: I could get in touch with my contact at the DMV and have them run the plate, or I could talk to Sgt. Barrows at LAPD and see if there's been any stolen cars reported over the last few days. If this was a kidnapping, there's a decent chance the car was stolen.

The next morning, I call Barrows at LAPD. "Hey Jim, this is René with Pierson Investigations. I'm wondering if you've had any blue Caravans reported as stolen in the last week or so. I have a client whose car is missing."

"Sure, let me check," he responds. After a couple of minutes, he replies, "Yes, as a matter of fact. License plate JLM 664. Reported stolen last week. Wait—it was found three days ago on Fairfax Avenue. It's been towed to the impound lot, no keys were found. I can email you the report?"

"That would be great, really appreciate it," I tell him. I pick up the email on my phone and call the owner, a Stewart Billings living in Hermosa Beach. He answers. "Mr. Billings? This is René Sinclair with Pierson Investigations. I understand your van was stolen recently, and recovered. I'm trying to run down the person responsible for the theft. Will you be picking it up from the LAPD impound lot soon?"

"Yes, I wanted to pick it up on my lunch break today."

"I wanted to inspect the inside for any possible clues as to who might have done this. How about this; I'll pick you up and give you a ride to the lot, if you'll let me look over the inside. What do you think?"

"Sure, that sounds good. I get a break at 12:30. Pick me up at Wilson's Mechanical on 34th Street in Hermosa," he says.

"I'll be there," I tell him.

I pick him up and we drive to the impound lot. Once there, he shows the attendant his ID, and we're escorted to the van. "I'll meet you out front," I yell out as he starts up the van. He pulls up on the street, behind where I parked, and I walk over. "This shouldn't take long," I assure him.

"Okay," he says.

The van is kind of a trash bin on wheels, so I find an empty bag and start collecting the debris. "Is it okay if I keep this stuff? You never know what can come from the smallest things."

"Yeah, take it," he responds.

In the very back, next to a spare tire mounted against the sidewall, is a woman's ring with a jade stone mounted in silver. He isn't aware of this find, so I think I'll keep it to myself for now. When I'm through with my tour de garbage, I thank him and we both head out.

I drive back to the office to see what items of interest I can discover from the van. The ring, of course, so I'll have to check with the mom to verify that it's Gina's. I dig through the goody bag of trash, finding junk food wrappers, paper coffee cups, and a variety of paper receipts. One stands out. It's from Bob's Burger Palace in Manhattan Beach, with a time and date stamp of 12:30 a.m. the night of the abduction. Some drive-throughs have security cameras at the checkout window; maybe I'll get lucky.

I drive down to Manhattan to get a burger. I get a Double-Trouble, basically two of everything a burger can hold, and at the window, mounted about six feet high just as you exit the drive-through, is a video camera. I park in the lot and go inside.

After a couple of heart-stopping bites, I catch my breath and walk up to the inside counter. "Could I please speak to your manager? No complaints just need a word."

The guy at the front says, "Sure." After a couple minutes, he comes back out with the manager.

"How can I help you?" he asks.

"I have a favor to ask. I'm investigating a recent auto theft, and I have reason to believe the thief came through your drive-through." I hand him our business card. "I have the time and date it would have happened. I can give you a hundred dollars for a look at your video feed around that time."

He kind of thinks for a moment, then says, "Sure, come through here." He leads me through the kitchen to a room in the back. "It's all digital, so we should be able to find something," he offers. He sits down at his desk and brings up the app that runs his video cameras.

I hand him the receipt and tell him, "Here's his receipt. Bring up the date and time, if you would." He scrolls through that day's footage, then comes to the timeframe. "Start a couple minutes before?" I ask. As we watch, a couple cars pass through, then bingo, the blue van. I can make out the license plate, and it matches. As the van pulls to the checkout window, you can see the driver pretty clearly. "Stop there!" I yell out. "Can you screenshot that frame?"

"Sure," he replies.

"Could you put that image on this thumb drive for me?"

"No problem," and he transfers the JPEG to my drive on his computer.

"That's perfect, here you go," and I hand him the hundred dollars. As we walk out, I say to him, "Thanks again. Great burgers, by the way," and I pick up the remains of the burger off my table and walk out.

My hope is to convince my cop buddy Lt. Garrison, Jim, to use the facial recognition software at LAPD. At this point, I'll have to bring him in on the auto-theft investigation, but I have no real evidence of a kidnapping yet.

"Hey Jim, it's René. I've got something you might be able to help me with. Can I come by in a little while?"

"No problem, let's make it an hour," he replies.

"Great, see you then."

This will be a little tricky. I'll have to explain how I got the receipt and how I knew about the stolen van. I also don't want him to push too hard on this, because if this guy comes up on the recognition program, I don't want him picked up until I know more about the possible kidnapping.

Walking into the police station is always a bit intimidating. It's that feeling of guilt, those times you stole a candy bar or ran a red light, mixed in with the macho vibe cops tend to give out. There's no doubt I respect what they do; their job is underappreciated and underpaid. Jim's desk is upstairs, and as I arrive, I see some other civilians looking like they wished they were somewhere else.

"Hey, how's biz?" he asks.

"You know, cheating men, divorcing women, the usual," I respond. "How about you?"

"Dead people, missing cats, and a couple more calls from your ex, the usual," he responds.

"Good luck with that last one. Wear protection." This brings a couple laughs from the guys next to us.

"I ran down a possible perp on a stolen vehicle you guys recovered. The owner let me look through his car and I found a fast-food receipt that was transacted that same day. The manager let me review some video footage from a security cam, and I got an image of a guy in what appears to be the stolen car. Could we run your facial recognition software on this guy to see if he's in the system, maybe has a record? Not sure, but he may be linked to another case I'm working on."

"We can try it, but we'll have to have more to go on before I can open a file on him."

"No problem, I'm just trying to add some pieces to the puzzle." I hand him the thumb drive and we go across the room to an office full of computers, including LAPD security-cam monitors and large screens divided into multiple images of the city government buildings. Jim sits down at one of the stations, inserts the thumb drive, and starts the software. The whole process can take a while, so he suggests we get some coffee and a donut out front, saying "That's all we do here, but times have changed. No more hanging out at the donut shops—we have them delivered!"

"As long as you've got the kind with the little sprinkles, your secret's good with me," I tell him. The donuts are stale and the coffee cold, but we indulge anyway.

"Let's go back to my desk; I'm having the results sent there." There's a notification on his computer. "Here you go: Daniel Bergman. Two priors for B&E and a conviction in Florida for felony assault, and it looks like he did eight months for that one. Sounds like an upstanding citizen, might have a future in politics!"

I glance through his profile. Caucasian, thirty-six, two hundred and twenty pounds, and a last known address in Korea Town, LA.

"I can't give you a printout of this, but if you want to make a couple notes, go ahead," Jim tells me.

"I'm going to check this guy out. If I get any more info on him, I'll give you a call."

"Yep. Tread lightly with this guy. I see one of his last known associates is Darius McCabe. Not a nice guy," he cautions me. I don't know the name, but if Jim does, I believe him.

Driving back to the office, I get a call from Gloria. "Oh my God, she's been kidnapped! I just got a call from someone demanding ten million dollars." Her voice is breathless, and I can tell she's stressing out.

"Where are you? I have an idea who might be involved, but let's not talk over the phone. Can you come to the office?" I ask her.

"Yes, please help! Will they hurt her? I can be there in half an hour."

"They can't risk hurting her; they just want money. Don't panic. I'll see you in a half an hour."

Now things have stepped up a level. I'm just getting to the office when we hang up. I jump on the computer and do a little research on our Mr. Bergman. Looks like he works as a security guard at the Dew Drop Inn, a strip joint downtown. The club owner is, yep, you guessed it, Darius McCabe. I was wondering what I was going to do tonight; sorry, Netflix. McCabe also has an import business, with a warehouse in Encino. His finances are way in the red with outstanding debts and back taxes. I'm guessing he could be looking for an influx of cash—say, ten million?

Gloria knocks at the door and Theo responds quickly. I meet the cat at the door and pick him up. No escaping this time, buddy.

She is in a panic, bloodshot eyes and shaking with nervousness. "What's going to happen? You've got to do something!" she says, barely able to speak.

"Come in, come in. Sit down, I'll get you a glass of water," I tell her. On cue, Theo jumps into her lap, which startles her, but she makes room and begins petting him. I hand her the water and sit at the desk. "Tell me exactly what they said to you."

"They said, 'We have your daughter; you have forty-eight hours to come up with ten million dollars. No police or she dies. I'll call back with details,' and he hung up."

"Okay, we can get through this. At this point, we can't afford to involve the police. I have a good idea who did this, but I need another day to verify a few things. If you have access to the money, you should have it ready just in case, but I don't think it'll come down to that. You need to stick with your regular routines, and for now keep this between us. The goal is to get your daughter back before the forty-eight hours is up and bust this guy, or guys. Don't call me on your regular cell phone. Buy one of those pay-per-use phones. Here's my personal number, call it. I will involve the police when it's safe for your daughter."

She seems to be a little calmer, and for once Theo had been useful. She sets Theo down and we walk toward the door. "Are you okay to drive?" I ask.

"Yes, I think so," she says.

"Get that phone today and call me. They won't hurt her. They can't risk doing anything to keep them from getting paid."

"Alright, I'll call you soon," and she walks to the stairs.

That night, I head for the Dew Drop Inn. After a quick passing of the wane, the doorman lets me in. It's the typical scene, a girl on stage, a few others doing the rounds looking for a lap dance, and a fair share of lowlifes spread around, hooting and getting plowed. I take a seat near a dark corner and survey the place. To the right of the stage is a hallway leading to a back room, and standing at the entrance is Mr. Bergman. It doesn't take long before a young lady approaches me with a smile. "Can you buy me a drink?" she asks.

"Sure." I wave down a waitress.

"Shirley Temple please, and for the gentleman?" she asks.

"Scotch rocks."

"Can I interest you in a dance? I can keep it warm," referring to, well, you know.

"I'll give you a hundred dollars, but I just have a few questions," I tell her. She scoots her chair next to mine and puts her hand in my lap. She holds her other hand out, wanting the hundred up front. I hand her the hundred and look her in the eye. "Can we go back there?" I ask pointing to the hallway.

"Oh no, I don't think Danny would like that," she says.

"If there's a room back there, I could come up with a lot more than a hundred."

"That's where the boss works, but we could go to your car," she responds.

"Is Darius still the boss here?" I ask her.

"Ever since I started, five months ago."

"Is Danny still doing that import business?" I ask her.

She looks a little curious now, so I'd better not probe any deeper. "It's Darius's business, Danny is just the manager. Why?" she asks.

"I do some importing myself, you know, antiques, jewelry, and a few other things," hoping this would satisfy her curiosity.

"Oh nice. Should we go out to your car?"

"I Ubered here, but what time do you get off? Maybe we could get a hotel."

"I'm off at two. That sounds good."

"Here's another fifty. Would you pay the waitress for the drinks and keep the rest for yourself?" I ask her.

"Sure, see you later," she says.

I get up and head out. When I ran Danny through my search tools, I found he owns a 2016 Lexus sedan. It's parked in the lot. I put a GPS tracker under his rear bumper, magnetized to the frame. Now I can track his movements on my phone and get alerts every time he moves.

The next morning, I dig into Darius's business contacts and the location of his warehouse. I drive out to the warehouse to check out the security and general layout. It's located in a business district, but most of the area is plagued with run-down older buildings on large unkempt lots. I park down the street and walk down the sidewalk to the fenced lot, secured by a locked gate. The building is a three-story structure set about a hundred feet back from the gate entrance. There are a number of large semi trucks being loaded with boxes and various items from within the warehouse. It looks like the place is being cleaned out. I don't want to be seen, so I walk back to my car and leave the area.

That night, I go back to the warehouse to take a better look. I get there just after dark, and as I approach the area, a single car is just leaving, and the driver locks the gate behind him. I climb the fence on the far north side of the lot, an area that's unlit by the building's security lights. On the side of the building, I find a door that's secured by a combination lock. I brought some lock cutters and easily cut the lock.

The inside is dimly lit, and I can't see any security cams mounted on the walls. It's an open structure with a twenty-five-foot-high ceiling, and on the opposite side are some rooms and a staircase leading to an office on the second floor. I go through the first-floor rooms, but they're empty.

I climb the stairs to check out the upper office, and I think I can smell natural gas as I get higher. I open the office door and flip on the light. The room is also empty, and suddenly someone slams the door shut. It's been locked from the outside. I try to knock it open with my shoulder, but it won't budge.

Then I hear an explosion. Smoke starts leaking through the bottom of the door, and the room will quickly be filled and unbreathable. I get out my lock cutters and go to work on the door hinges. I first try cutting through the metal hinges, but it doesn't work. Finally, I jam the cutters into the door cracks just above hinges and pull down several times. This is working, and I pop off the screws that secure the hinges to the wall. I get a second hinge off, and I'm able to push the door open enough to slip out.

By this time, the smoke is thick, and the place is engulfed in flames. I make it down the stairs and look for an escape. There are windows about six feet off the floor. I push a crate over to one of the windows, climb on top of it, and smash the window with the cutters. I jump out and land on the concrete outside of the building. It wasn't a well-executed jump, and my left ankle lets me know it.

I run from the building and can hear the sound of fire trucks wailing in the distance. I make an awkward climb back over the fence and hobble back to my car and jump in, taking off in the opposite direction from the sirens I could hear closing in. My hope of discovering Gina in the warehouse has been quickly extinguished. I have to assume someone had seen me casing the warehouse earlier in the day and had hoped to trap me in the inferno they'd already planned. This explained why the place was cleared out earlier in the day. I'm guessing they hope to collect insurance money from the fire, blaming it on a gas leak. Time is running out, and it's time to get the police involved.

The next morning, I call Jim and tell him I have a case for him. He'll be in at 10:00 a.m., so I tell him I'll be in right away. Then I get a notification from the GPS monitor I had put on Danny's car. He's in San Fernando on a street in the foothills of the valley. What is he doing out there? He lives in LA. That might be worth checking out.

I meet up with Jim at the station and lay out the situation. I tell him I've tracked Danny to a house in the valley. He talks to his superior and gets the green light to raid the house, and they'll be securing a search warrant immediately. Within twenty minutes we get the warrant, and a SWAT team is assembled for the mission. On the drive out, I call Gloria and tell her what's up. She's anxious, of course, and I promise I'll call her once things have developed.

As we arrive in the area, a helicopter flying at a fairly high altitude describes the scene. The house is set back on a large parcel and is a one-story structure with a small footprint. The SWAT vehicle pulls up first and quickly secures the area. We come in behind them and stay back behind the SWAT team. The team leader has been briefed about a possible kidnapping and is to proceed as if it's a hostage situation. Danny's car is parked alongside the small house, which looks like it's a hundred years old, with steps leading up to a front porch.

The SWAT leader comes through on the bullhorn. "Daniel Bergman, this is the LAPD. We have a warrant for your arrest. Step out with your hands in the air."

A rifle peers out from a front window and opens fire. The team doesn't return fire, standard procedure when a hostage may be inside. Once again, the team leader announces, " Come out with your hands up. This is your last warning." More shots fly out, ricocheting off the vehicles and whining through the air.

The decision is made to use tear gas to force him out. A SWAT team member sneaks up from the side of the house, climbs onto the porch, and throws a tear gas grenade through the glass window. We can hear coughing from inside, and after a couple minutes, Danny comes through the front door, bent over, holding his chest, and coughing. He still has his rifle in his left hand, and the SWAT leader yells out, "Drop the gun and put your hands up!" Danny raises the gun as if to fire, and a barrage of bullets brings him down quickly.

Once he's secured, two team members enter the house cautiously. In a minute, one of the team members comes back out the front door. "All clear, hostage secured." I run up to the front, and the officer helps Gina out of the house, slightly coughing from the leftover smoke.

"Gina? I'm René. Are you hurt?" I ask.

"No, just . . ." and she can't say any more. I put my arm around her shoulder and help her to our car. She's crying at this point, so I try my best to console her. I give her a water bottle and stand by her while she regains her composure.

After a few minutes, Jim returns to the car. "We will need to question you about what happened, but let's just get you home for now," he tells her.

"Your mother hired me to see if you were okay. I guess you two text daily. I told her I'd call her when I heard any news about your disappearance." I called Gloria.

"Gloria?"

"Yes?"

"Gina is safe. She's here with me, I'll put her on." I hand the phone to Gina.

"Mom?"

"Yes, sweetheart. Are you okay? I've been worried sick about you."

"I'm okay. Miss you." At that point, I slide back and let them talk.

I have Jim drive us to Gloria's house. When we arrive, Gloria comes running out and hugs Gina. "Are you two good?" I ask. No response is a response. They walk arm in arm into the house.

I feel like I did good. Sometimes, things go right. This was one of those times.

One Love From The
Piano
KEITH ALLAN

One Love From The Piano

By

Keith Allan

One Love From The Piano

"You have a request," mentioned the club manager.

I spun half way around the piano bench and bent over out of the light. "We talked about this; I don't do requests."

"I know, I know, but this is different. You see that lady across the way, sitting near the table under those green neon lights? She's the club owner's wife- a big fan of yours. She wanted me to give you this (he handed me a hundred-dollar bill). She just wants one song, and she said there's another C-note for you if you would join her after your set, no strings."

"Okay, no problem. What does she want me to play?"

"A Waltz for Debbie."

One of my favorites from the genius of Bill Evans. I kind of follow his chord patterns and improvise my own melody. This was no ordinary nightclub. It is located on the top floor of an eighteen-story business building, right off Wilshire Blvd. It's a members-only club, and you need an access card to get up the elevator. They have me play Monday and Tuesday nights, and the clientele is made up of LA's elite- movie moguls, celebrities, actors, and other nefarious types that look like mafia kingpins- West Coast style. I was playing in a trio in a Venice jazz club, more of a dive than a club really. This gig came about when the manager approached me and asked about doing some off nights at an exclusive club in Bel Air. He asked if I'd ever heard of Les Trois Amants. I told him no. He said it would be a solo gig, and I could play any style I wanted; it would be more in the realm of background music. The first couple nights would be a sort of an audition. I would have to leave my phone at the door, and the clientele's privacy was extremely important. Whatever I heard or saw would never leave the building, and I would need to sign a contract, to that effect. The pay was good, so I decided to give it a whirl. This place was way out of my league- only top-shelf liquor, an interior design you would only find in Bel Air, a Steinway grand piano, and the waitresses were aspiring actresses and Vogue-type models. This was a dream gig- amazing atmosphere, good pay, and I could play whichever style I wanted. I guess I passed the audition, because they kept me around.

After I finished my set, I went to the bar, grabbed some ice water and made my way over to her table.

"Hello, I'm Angelica, but please call me Angie." She held out her hand in the manner of a princess, and I awkwardly shook it like a cowboy, not a prince.

"I'm Renee, it's a pleasure to meet you". I sat down across from her, and there was a moment of silence when she smiled pleasantly, but in a coy way as if she had a secret. Her accent told me she was French, but with a firm grasp of the English language.

"Thank you for the song, I love the way you play. I'm having a party at my house this Saturday night, and I would love to have you over You would be a guest, and not required to perform. I want to introduce you to some of my friends, and I have a job proposal I would like to offer you".

"I'm afraid I might seem out of place; I'm not a very social person."

She laughed, "That's all right, I like that about you."

"May I ask the nature of your job proposal?" I asked.

"Let's just say I can help you with your tuition and housing expenses in the fall, I believe your grant is nearing its end? It will also give you the opportunity to travel abroad this summer, if that's of interest to you. But please, come to the party and I can explain. Oh, here's my husband's tailor's card. Jean Paul is quite good. Get whatever you'd like, and tell him Angie sent you and the event is black-tie. I'll call him in the morning, and let him know you're coming in the afternoon."

As she slid the card across the table, I reached for it, and she placed her hand on top of mine. "Please come, love; it'll be fun!"

With that she got up, flashed that secret smile, and walked towards the elevator. As she did, two rather large well-dressed gentleman rose from an adjacent table, and followed her out. I'm assuming they were some sort of security personnel, judging by their stoic demeanor and deliberate gait.

Okay, so what just happened? How did she know about my grant? I'm not exactly in the first ten hits on Google. I kind of sat there, staring into nowhere, when the club manager approached me.

"Quite a lady, don't you think?"

I snapped out of my stupor, looked up and replied, "Yes, but kind of a mystery".

"She's the one that saw you playing in your trio and got you this gig. I don't need to know what she wanted, but whatever it is, please try and accommodate her; it will benefit both of us. Her husband owns the building, among other things, so watch what you say and do, he can change your life for better or worse."

Now I needed a drink, and I don't drink often. A curious blend of confusion, expectation, and trepidation swirled through my head as I sat at the bar stirring a scotch that needed no mixing.

I always run through the pluses and minuses of new propositions, almost to the level of a person with OCD. I'm quite ordinary, really, so when the extraordinary presents itself I find myself in a quandary. I have always wondered how the other half lives; this might be my ticket. Okay! I'm gonna do it.

The next morning, I finished some work on my thesis, and emailed the results to my professor. Summer was an opportunity to do some independent research, and take a break from the stress of grad school. At about 2:00, I went to the address on the card Angie had given me. It was a small but elegantly-detailed shop off of Rodeo Drive. As I came through the door, and a little bell attached to it announced my presence, an older gentleman greeted me. "Welcome Monsieur, my name is Jean Paul. How may I help you?"

"My name is Renee..." and before I could finish my sentence, he interrupted with "Ah, yes! Angelica told me you'd be coming. I have some lovely choices for you. Please, follow me." He was a small man, a little pudgy but full of energy.

I told him it was a black-tie occasion, but I wanted something non-descript, yet appropriate for such an event. He suggested a simple tuxedo, but with beautiful attention to details, and suggested a white dress shirt and black bow tie. I've never been fitted for a suit; I was beginning to feel entitled...not really, ha ha. He said he doesn't often suggest shoes, but then he came out of the back room with some traditional wingtips. Those fit well, so I thanked him and told him they would do just fine. He told me the tux would be ready by Friday afternoon, and it was a pleasure to work with me.

As I left, I think he could tell this was a new experience for me, not just the fitting but also the crowd I would be mingling with. "Don't worry sir, you will do just fine."

“Thank you, Jean Paul.” And as I left the shop, I turned and showed him a crossed middle and index finger.

On Friday, I returned to the shop, and Jean Paul greeted me with a smile. “Please, come try it on.”

I went into a dressing room and was handed the suit and shoes. As I left the room, Jean Paul walked with me to a nearby mirror. He had me turn to him before I could get a look at the new me, and he adjusted my bow tie, straightened the jacket’s lapel, and lightly brushed the front of the coat for lint. I turned towards the mirror and was a bit shocked by what I saw. It might have been similar to the feeling when a bride-to-be sees herself in her wedding dress for the first time, although scaled back a bit.

“Bond, James Bond,” and I laughed at myself. “You look magnificent, Monsieur Sinclair, you will be quite well received, I have no doubt”.

“You really are amazing. This has exceeded my expectations, and I can’t thank you enough”.

“I will let you change,” and he slightly bowed and waved his left hand back towards the changing room.

As I left the shop, I tried to hand him one of the hundred-dollar bills Angie had given me, but he wouldn’t accept it. “No, no that is not necessary. Angelica and her husband are wonderful clients, and she has taken care of everything. Have a beautiful day!”

Later that afternoon I got an e-invite to the party. I wasn’t sure how Angie got my email address, but I’m guessing she knows more about me than I can imagine.

When I pulled up to the address of the party, a guard that approached my car with a smile greeted me. "Your name, sir?" he asked.

"Renee Sinclair"

He scrolled through a tablet device, found my name and replied, "Follow the road up the hill, when you get to the fork go right". He returned to his guard shack and the gate opened.

When I got through the fork, a valet again stopped me. "Take this slip, and when you leave the party we will bring your car down. Just follow the stairs up to the house. Have a great night!"

The 'house' looked more like a 5-star resort. It had several levels, projecting out over the hillside. It reminded me of a multistory Frank Lloyd Wright design; modern, with mid-century style. As I walked up the lit pathway, there were several opportunities to branch to my left to access what I assume were different parts of the house. Fortunately, there were little 'Party' signs posted, that kept me going in the right direction.

Arriving at my destination, I was again greeted, this time by a beautiful young woman holding a tray of champagne. "Welcome! Champagne?"

I'm not much of a champagne drinker, but I accepted her offer, she was difficult to refuse. "Thank you".

The entrance was quite spectacular, with an assortment of artwork including paintings, sculptures, and some three-dimensional creations constructed of wood, metal, plastic, and other materials I couldn't immediately identify. The entry room had a high ceiling, with occasional steps up or down, separating parts of the room. The room extended to a massive deck that overlooked the city of Bel Air. There were several guests milling about, and a few very recognizable celebrities.

I glanced to my left and caught the eye of one of my professors.

"Renee! Come over here, I want you to meet some people".

I was amazed that I would know anyone at the party, and Professor Reynolds was maybe the last person I expected to see. I joined his group. As I did, he put a hand on my shoulder and began introductions. "This is Renee Sinclair, one of the bright young minds of the mathematics department. This is Tomas Winston...Lyle Montrose...and Carla Jacobs".

I shook hands and said "Hi, hi, nice to meet you."

Tomas spoke up "What are you working on Renee?"

"I'm just trying to finish my thesis, nothing too revolutionary I'm afraid".

"He's just being modest. Renee's work could transform particle theory and greatly benefit solar energy collection and storage" Professor Reynolds added.

"Well, I still have a few obstacles to overcome, so, we'll see how it goes," I said with a bit of a chuckle.

I had read about Lyle Montrose in last month's Forbes. He was an industrialist that claimed to be converting to a carbon-free, zero emissions production environment, but was receiving a lot of pushback from various watch groups. He was being called out for not meeting his targeted CO2 output levels he had promised. "Are you here to save the world, Renee?" he said.

"No, I just work on the theory end, not its application. I'm not a green mathematician; I don't want to be defined by a color, although in today's political climate, it's almost unavoidable," I responded.

"Sadly, that's the inconvenient truth," the professor added.

Carla turned towards me "And I thought all mathematicians were boring, save you professor. We should have lunch at the university sometime, Renee. My department is full of pudgy old fuddy-duddies, over-read, and educated beyond their intelligence".

We all laughed and I responded, "I'd like that!"

At that moment Angie came up from my side and put her arm through mine. "I'm afraid I'm going to have to steal him away from you, I need to get him a real drink." With that she escorted me to the bar and said, "What would you like?" "Scotch please", "the single malt Teddy," she added. "How do you like the party?"

"I'm in a world I'm unfamiliar with, but I always wanted to visit other planets."

And she laughed.

"I really appreciate you inviting me, and your home is amazing. Do you ever feel claustrophobic being here?" I said jokingly.

She laughed again, "Actually yes, in a strange way. I love to travel; LA can be a bit too much for me." "That brings me to the reason I wanted you to come. I'm going on a trip in a few days, and I'd like you to come. I travel with a small group of people, and I think you would fit in nicely. I have a role for everyone, but you would also have a lot of free time to yourself."

"Why me, and what would be my role? I do occasionally participate in role-playing."

She seemed to like my twisted sense of humor. "Playing the piano at times, and I understand you do some photography?"

"Yes, but it's more of a hobby," I confessed.

"Also, my fifteen-year-old nephew will be joining us, and he's obsessed with surfing. I understand this is another one of your hobbies, and according to Billabong, you had a future in the sport."

"A short future might be more accurate."

"Well, one of our stops will be in the Mentawai Islands, and I'd like you to keep an eye on him out there. He's rather precocious, and having an adult accompany him would help relieve my stress level, and his mom's."

"I've never really thought of myself as a responsible adult, to be honest."

"I trust you, and I don't trust many people," she replied. "We will be gone about a month. Stopovers in Hawaii, Sydney, and Perth, where we will take my yacht north to Indonesia and the Mentawais". "From there, we may stop in Bangkok, unless I can wrap up my business there over the computer". "What do you think? Up for a little adventure?"

"Sounds like fun, but are you sure you have the right person for this?"

"Absolutely! I have a variety of character flaws, but I am a good judge of people. Also, I would pay you $10,000, and pay for your tuition and living expenses next year."

This definitely added to the pot. I had been wondering how I was going to survive next year.

"Will your husband be joining us?" I asked.

"He's in Sydney, so yes for a portion of the trip."

"I would need a passport and the required immunizations."

"I can take care of that, you can see my doctor, and I can expedite the passport process". "We would leave in a week. I have a very comfortable little jet, and the flight crew is outstanding."

"Okay, it does sound like fun. And I'll need a "How I spent my summer vacation' story for Carla in the fall."

This generated another laugh, and she replied, "Great, it's all settled then. I'll email you with all the details, but feel free to call me anytime, here's my personal number", and she handed me a business card that just said Angelica, and the number.

"Do many people say no to you?" I asked.

"Once in a while, but it doesn't bother me, I'm a big girl." No doubt. "By the way, you look enchanting in that tux!"

"Thank you, I don't recognize myself," I added.

"Now please, mingle. I might grab you now and then to have you meet some of my friends. Is that okay?"

"Of course, feel free."

I couldn't help but feel like an outsider, so my form of mingling was more like hiding. As I walked out on the deck, I could hear music coming from the level below. I saw a couple walking down a flight of stairs off the left side of the deck, so I decided I would follow them. On the lower deck there was a large pool, and a jazz quintet playing at the far end of the deck. There were tables and chairs set up for the guests, and a bar adjacent to where the group was playing. The quintet was quite good, playing a Getz/Gilberto tune, and the female singer had a style reminiscent of Flora Purim, one of my favorite female vocalists. This looked like a good hiding place, so I took a table on the perimeter of the area.

I guess I wasn't quite invisible enough, because after a few songs Angie approached my table. "I thought you might find your way down here. How do you like the group?"

"They sound great. You know I love Latin jazz, and it's hard to find a singer that sings in Portuguese, especially in this part of the world."

"Would you like to meet her? She's quite lovely."

"Sure, maybe when they finish this set?"

"Yes, of course," and she took a chair next to me.

We chatted about the upcoming trip, and a few of her guests stopped by our table to say hello. She was the type of person that diverts the attention she receives and includes those around her in conversation. I've met a couple celebrities at the club, and it's always refreshing to find one so full of grace and truly interested in others and what's new in their lives.

When the group finished their set, Angie walked me over to the band area and called out "Estrela!"

The girl looked in her early twenties, with a shy demeanor, and rather a frail appearance. She smiled softly, and in almost a whisper said, "Si, madam".

"This is my friend, Renee. He's a pianist and would like to meet you."

Angie replied in broken English, "Play piano?"

"A little yes. You have a beautiful voice."

"Thank you, sir" she said in a humble way.

"You two should play a duet!" Angie interjected.

Estrela looked a little confused. The bass player had overheard our conversation and translated it into Portuguese.

"Yes, if you would like." Estrela had said to the bass player in Portuguese, which he translated back to us.

"I don't want to intrude; I'm enjoying the group's songs."

"It's no intrusion, you two would make a great duo. Renee, why don't you pick a song in their genre, and see if Estrela would know it."

I wasn't in a position to say no, so I thought for a moment and said, "Do you know 'Meditacao' (meditation)?"

"Si, eu amo isso!" she answered with a broader smile.

I was reluctant to say much more, I don't speak Portuguese and her English was limited. I waved an open hand in the direction of the piano, took a small bow, and smiled. The song has no real introduction, but it's important to establish the key, so I played three chords that would let her know what note to start on. She picked up on my cue, and we were off. I was so enthralled with her voice, having rarely played with a singer. I had to keep reminding myself to focus on the piano. I kept my arrangement simple, and let her style carry the song. She would occasionally look back at me, smile, and look back at the audience, although her eyes were often closed, and her expression was as if she was in meditation. As a huge fan of Antonio Carlos Jobim, I can't tell you how gratifying it was to play one of his songs, with a talented and sensual Portuguese singer. Scratch that off my bucket list. When we finished, there was an applause from the audience, and a number of people rose from their chairs. She took a gracious bow, then turned towards me, and I stood up from the piano bench and gave a half bow.

After the applause, I walked up to Estrela, took her left hand, and gave it a soft kiss. "Thank you, you were wonderful," I added.

She looked at me with a big smile and replied, "Love your play!"

Angie was beaming, and grabbed both of our hands "That was breathtaking". I walked with Angie back to our table and we both sat down.

"I was almost in tears during the song, and I only know a little Portuguese" and she laughed. "Duets are my favorite, and you two had a chemistry that vibrated through the air". "She's really an artist. There's a passion in her voice that is rare, and I had a hard time focusing on the tune; I just wanted to watch her and listen". "I knew you would like her. You two will have to stay in touch, maybe even write together. I'm envious of your talents, but I enjoy taking a small role in nurturing young artists or at least bringing them into the public eye". "I need to greet a couple of guests that should be arriving any time, shall we go upstairs?"

"Of course," I replied.

Once upstairs, I excused myself, "Excuse me a minute". And I headed for the restroom. It was really just a reason to give her time with her guests. I like being in this environment, just for the experience. That's not to say I was the least bit comfortable, but being in unfamiliar settings teaches you things about people. After about an hour, I started to run out of places to hang out, and needed an exit. I would have to say goodbye to Angie, so I strolled around until I spotted her talking with a couple of actors I recognized. They were what I would call Hollywood outcasts, the type that speaks their mind at the expense of their careers. I approached the group and quietly came into Angie's view.

"Renee, you must meet a couple friends of mine- this is Edward Rollins and Tyler Thorn. This is Renee Sinclair- exceptional pianist and grad student at UCLA".

"Hi Renee, are you playing tonight...the piano I mean?"

"No, well I did play one song. I've seen both of you in a couple of films. Very nice to meet you."

"How did you meet Angie?" Tyler asked.

"I work at Les Trois Amants a couple nights a week. We met there".

"You two should come on a Monday or Tuesday night and hear Renee play, he's quite brilliant and with a unique blend of jazz styles."

"She's overselling me I'm afraid, but Angie has been very helpful with my piano life". "Thank you so much for inviting me, such a lovely party. I'm trying to get an early start tomorrow, so I'll be taking off."

"Thank you so much for coming! And that song with Estrela was a joy. I'm so looking forward to our trip. Drive safe!"

"I will, thanks again". "Nice meeting you" and I made eye contact with Edward and Tyler. I found the entryway and made my way back to the parking area. A valet brought my car around and I headed out.

Driving down Mulholland is kind of like Mr.Toad's Ride at Disneyland; a series of tight curves and switchbacks. As I came around a corner, I saw a car that had run off the road and settled in a ditch. There was smoke coming from the front of the car, and its lights were on and the motor running. I pulled over and ran over to the driver's side. The driver was slumped over the wheel, and apparently unconscious. I knocked on the door's glass window, and the driver looked up at me, still resting his head on the steering wheel. It was the bass player from the party!

I motioned for him to roll down his window. Once it got part way down, I said, "Don't move, I'm calling 911." He seemed to acknowledge what I'd said, so as I made the call, I walked around to the passenger side. Sitting there, and looking rather shook was Estrela. She looked uninjured, so I opened her door and said "Are you okay?"

She looked up at me and said, "Si, acho que sim".

I helped her out of the car, and walked her around to the back of the car. She was still in shock, so I helped her lean against the trunk of the car, supporting her with my right arm around her shoulder.

"Help is coming," I told her, hoping she would understand.

"Martin, Martin!" she exclaimed.

"I think he's okay," I told her.

Within a few minutes the police arrived, followed by an ambulance. They set up cones and flairs around the perimeter, and the paramedics attended to Martin. I could see Martin would be taken to the ER, and as they put him on the gurney, Estrela walked over to the paramedics. She looked very concerned, and the officer in charge approached her and said, "One of our officers can give you a ride home".

"She doesn't speak too much English, but I'm an acquaintance of hers and can give her a ride." Estrela looked at the policeman, then back at me. I motioned with my hands like I was driving, then pointed to her and then me, and made a little air picture of a house. She slightly smiled through her grief-stricken facial expression, and nodded her head.

He took down her information off of her ID card, then turned to me and added, "Tell her we may have a couple questions for her later."

"Of course," I said. With my arm over her shoulders, I walked her over to the passenger-side of my car. I helped her in, shut the door, then went around and got in.

"What's your address?" I asked.

She understood and handed me her ID card. She lived in Santa Monica, not too far from me. We pulled out from the accident scene and headed for her place. When we got there, I was a bit surprised at the house we drove up to. There was a walkway on the side of the property. When we got out of the car, she took my hand and led me down the walkway to a small guesthouse in the back. She unlocked the door, then turned to me and said, "Stay? Night?"

She was still very shaken from the ordeal, and I wasn't going to say no to her in the state she was in. "Okay".

We went inside the small one-bedroom guesthouse.

"We sleep now, okay?"

"Yes" I replied.

She changed into a nightgown and I arranged some pillows on the couch.

"No, bed?" she asked.

"Okay". There are times when your morals are tested, and though being in bed with a woman that just went through a traumatic experience shouldn't be one, I still had to remind myself not to take advantage. I removed my tux, pants, shirt and tie, and climbed into the bed next to her. She rolled on her side, scooted over next to me and put her hand on my chest. I placed my hand lightly on top of hers, and said, "Good night".

"Good night, Renee" she replied.

About 6:30 in the morning, I heard an alarm go off. I was still asleep, but after a couple of minutes I looked over and saw her putting on a maid's uniform.

"I go work, you sleep". "Done at 5:00, you call?" she added.

"Yes, I will". A part of me was upset that a woman of such talent was struggling to make a living, and not able to live off her voice. Jazz singers are quite familiar with this scenario, and in LA there is little work for jazz musicians these days; not in vogue, I guess. I got up shortly after she left for work and drove home.

I used most of the day planning for my trip. I got an email from Angie with an itinerary, and a list of steps I would need to follow, including how to secure my travel documents, and a doctor's appointment for the necessary shots I would need. She also left a note that she hoped I would be okay with taking the role of travel photographer occasionally. That afternoon I received a small padded envelope sent overnight. Inside was a gift card from Angie for five thousand dollars to one of LA's largest camera supply stores. She included a note saying, 'Please use this card to get whatever you need for your camera. If it's not enough please call me, Thanks, Angie'. This lady is thorough. I did need a mid-range telephoto lens, so later that afternoon, I picked one up.

Around 6:00, I called Estrela. "Would you like to go to dinner?" I had looked this up in Portuguese, though my vocalization was sketchy at best.

"Yes, please!" was her response.

"7:00?" I said.

"Yes," she confirmed.

She was ready to go when I arrived, and came to the door full of smiles.

"How are you?" I asked.

"Good, good," she replied.

"What type of food do you like? Thai, Chinese, Italian, Mexican, or something else?"

"All, you choose," she said.

I knew a great Thai place close by, so I said, "Thai!"

At the restaurant, I decided to try out my limited Spanish ability, knowing it has a lot of crossover with Portuguese. "Quieres algo de beber?" (Beer, wine, something else?)

"Wine, rojo," she responded.

I ordered our drinks, and after a few minutes of looking at the menu, we both ordered. She seemed to know something she liked, so I let her choose. Dinner was good, and since it was a warm late spring evening, I took her to the Santa Monica Pier. There's a lot going on out on the pier; rides, vendors, performers, restaurants, and a wide variety of characters ranging across every demographic. We spent much of our time laughing, and she had never been on a rollercoaster, so that was a must-do. The pier fishermen that were just wrapping up for the evening fascinated her. At one point, she grabbed my hand and started skipping along the wooden walkway, and I was obliged to follow in suit, although skipping isn't really my thing. She was a free spirit, the type that flourishes when unconfined, and just being around her set off an instinct to protect her from this crazy world. As we left the pier, we walked to a small bar just down from the beach. A couple more glasses of wine and the language barrier seemed to fade away. The mix of English, Spanish, and Portuguese became a laughing point in itself, and any opportunity to joke about it became mandatory. We drove back to her place and as she unlocked the front door, she grabbed my hand and pulled me in. She set down her keys, spun around, and drew me to her. I rested a hand on the side of her face, and we kissed. I must say, though I'm young and somewhat inexperienced, Latin women have a sensuality that touches the heart in a way that can't be put into words. I think it has to do with a mix of culture, confidence, and a sort of untamed instinct to connect to other people. She took the lead; I was the pawn and she the queen. I love this type of women; strong, confident, assertive yet very aware of their physical presence. There was no awkwardness to being with her, it was a matter of me letting go, and both responding to her and taking cues for when I would take control.

Another alarm at 6:30, and she was up, ready for work in no time. She came over to my side of the bed, kissed me, and as I started to get up, she put up her hand and said "Stay, sleep". This was an easy sell, I was barely awake and a little more sleep would be nice. I tried to go back to sleep, but my mind was on Estrela. Why now? Just when I meet someone, I could form a serious relationship with, I have to leave the country? They say timing is everything. Well, in this case bad timing. I know one thing that's for sure; I'll be spending as much time as possible over the next few days with Estrela. The trick will be explaining to her why I have to go on this trip, and how it's a way to help me get through grad school. I can tell this whole ordeal will be occupying my brain for a good time to come, in this country and the one's coming up.

With the exception of her working hours, we were together, like two peas in a pod. Dinners out, a little entertainment, and the rest of the night at her place or mine. It was now only five days until my trip, and I still hadn't mustered up the nerve to tell her, and what I would say.

It was midday when I got a call from Angie. She wanted to make sure everything for the trip was moving along as planned. At one point in the conversation, I mentioned I had been seeing Estrela. I explained the accident scene, and how things just progressed from there. There was a long pause in our talk, when she said, "Oh, I have an idea! Why don't we have Estrela join us part way through the trip! I'm thinking she could fly to Perth and come along on our yacht when we head north (a pause while she was thinking). Yes, so we'll spend about a week in Sydney, then fly to Perth for a week; at that point, we can fly her out and join us! Perfect! I have a ranch style home in Broome, and I'm planning a party for my diamond business partners in Southeast Asia. We have camels and horses, and you two would have a great time!"

"That sounds amazing, but she has work six days a week, and I'm not sure she can get out of it".

"That's not a problem. She works at the Beverly Hilton, and I'm good friends with Maggie, the manager. This will be fun! What do you think?"

"I'm good with it! It sounds incredible. I'll speak with Estrela tonight, she won't believe it".

When Estrela got home from work, I told her I had a surprise for her. There was a Mexican restaurant down the street, and one of the waiters spoke Portuguese. I wanted to make sure she was clear about the plan, so I told her we were having Mexican food tonight. Once we got there, I flagged down my buddy Antonio, and asked him if he could help us with some translations. After a couple of minutes, he came over and said, "Sure, how can I help?"

I first presented it as some good news and some bad news. The bad news first. I told her I had to go away for a couple of weeks. She looked horrified. Her mouth opened, and she reached across the table and took my hand.

"No," she pleaded. Then I told her to wait, there's some good news. (All this being translated) Angie is going to fly you to Australia in two weeks, where you'll join me and her group on her yacht. We will cruise north, stay at her ranch and visit some amazing places in Southeast Asia. She looked overwhelmed, and a bit confused. I could see her telling Antonio that she couldn't miss work, or something like that. I told him Angie would take care of that, you'll still have your job when you return. She still looked baffled. There were a few seconds of silence, when all of a sudden she jumped up, ran across to my side of the table and leaped into my lap, and started kissing me. When we came up for air, we were both smiling like we won the lotto. Antonio was smiling and said,

"Wow, that is so cool". She asked about her travel requirements, and I told her Angie could help, and would pay for her flight and incidentals.

After dinner, I called Angie and told her Estrela was a hundred percent up for it. She said "Yay! It's going to be a great trip! I'll call her boss in the morning and let her know". "Here's a friend of mine's number. Her name is Monique. She speaks Spanish so I think they'll be able to communicate fine. She will help Estrela with everything she needs, she's great".

"I can't tell you how much this means to me. You're a life-saver, really you are," I told her.

"Nonsense, what good is having money if you can't help make people's lives better, and what a great pair you two make. This is so exciting!" she said.

After the call, I told Estrela that everything was set, and tomorrow she should call Monique to help make the arrangements. I found an app on my phone that translates languages in real time, though a human translator does a much better job. Estrela understood enough of what I said to jump up and down, then leap into my arms and wrap her legs around my waist. We were at her place now, and together we hopped up and down in joy. There was a lot of preparation ahead, so I told her I would help while I was here but had to leave in five days. This didn't diminish her enthusiasm, and the rest of the night was celebration.

As the departure date approached, I hurried around the city, buttoning up loose ends, and notifying my primary professor. I would be able to work remotely on my thesis, but my professor told me there would be plenty of time to work on it when I returned, and I should enjoy my time away. That was good news, and a little break can give me a fresh perspective on some of the areas I'm working on.

The morning of my flight, I said goodbye to Estrela as she prepped for work. It was hard to leave each other, but I kept reminding her that we would be back together in two weeks. I drove home to finish packing for the trip. About 10:30, a large SUV pulled up and the driver came up to the house. "Hi I'm Jason, I'll be driving you to the airport". At the airport, we went through a security gate and drove onto the tarmac where a mid-size jet was being loaded with suitcases, and a few large containers. Angie was talking to a group of people next to the passenger entry, so I walked over to say hi. They were kind of lined up almost as if it were an inspection.

"Renee, let me introduce you to the crew. This is Marnie and Rochelle, our flight attendants, Jake and Mikhail, our security team, our copilot Mark, my good friends Jessica and Marissa, and my nephew Taylor. Everyone, this is Renee. He's the jazz pianist I told you about, as well as our in-house photographer. He'll also be Taylor's surf partner on the trip."

They all greeted me, and it seemed like they all knew each other the way they were joking around. We boarded the plane, taxied off the loading area, and took off.

The flight to Honolulu took about five hours, and once we got there, everyone but the flight crew took a private shuttle to a favorite restaurant of Angie's in town. Honolulu was just a stopover for refueling, so after our meal we re-boarded and took off for Sydney. We arrived at night time and took a twelve-seat van to a house that Angie stays at when she's there. After showing us to our rooms, the plan was to meet in the front entry room for drinks once we'd showered and changed. The whole group, including the flight crew, was very friendly and like Angie, they went out of their way to include me in their conversations. She went over the basic plans for the week, which included sightseeing, a night at the opera, some business meetings she would attend, and a couple days of free time. I was going to use that time to travel to the Gold Coast with Taylor to surf some of their renowned point breaks. I'd been to the area one other time with Billabong, and got a chance to surf Burleigh Heads, but I was hoping we'd get a few waves at Kirra or maybe Snapper Rocks.

The next morning, I rented a car, and Taylor and I headed north. I reminded him that Aussies are pretty aggressive in the water, and he would need to make sure he didn't take any waves that the locals wanted. We pulled up to Snapper, and the waves looked good. It's a little tricky staying clear of the rocks at low tide, so I suggested we move down the point a bit where there was a little deeper water. The wave can be really fast and it takes a while to figure out how to stay in front of it. We paddled out and worked our way into the lineup. I stayed close to Taylor in the beginning, until he got the hang of it. A good-looking wave came through, and a guy that caught it at the peak fell, so I yelled at Taylor to go for it. He dropped in, made a quick turn, and started pumping to keep up with it. A local guy took off in front of him and within a couple of seconds they collided and went down. I started paddling towards them as they both got back on their boards. The Aussie was yelling at Taylor, though it was his fault for interfering with Taylor's wave. He paddled towards Taylor, who was trying to play it cool. I got there just as a fight was about to ensue, and yelled at the local letting him know I was ready to step in if he started throwing punches. The local turned and saw me, and said something like 'fucking Americans', and started paddling back out.

Taylor said, "What's with that asshole! He dropped in on me".

"Yeah, I know, that was your wave, but the locals are kind of psycho towards outsiders. Nothing you can do about it". After about an hour we both got a few waves, and Taylor decided to move over the reef a bit farther. A set came in, and he took off on the first wave. It was pretty hollow, and he fell on the takeoff. It snapped his leash, and his board got carried in over some very shallow water. I could tell it was going to be difficult for him to get to it, so I paddled over and grabbed his board. I put one foot on the nose of his board, and paddled into deeper water towing his board out. This technique works fine until a wave comes, so I would have to jump off my board, wrap my arms around the nose of both boards, and duck-dive under the white water. Finally, we met up and I gave him his board. He had a couple cuts from the reef, but nothing serious. His leash was broken, so we decided to paddle in. Once on the shore, he thanked me, and we walked up the beach to our car. I called Angie, and told her we were getting a hotel for the night, so we could surf again in the morning. She was good with it, and asked if we were having fun. I didn't want to alarm her, so I said yes, but left out the less pleasant details.

The next morning, we went down to Burleigh Heads, and got some great surf. Not quite the long rides of Snapper, but less crowded and easier to manage. We surfed for four hours, and by the time we came in, we were completely drained of energy. We loaded up the car and headed back to Sydney. When we got home, it was about 6:00, so we showered and changed to go out to dinner with the group. At dinner, Taylor told the story about the local bully, and the swim-in over the rocks. I was worried Angie might be upset with what transpired, but Taylor made me out to be the hero, so everything was cool. I mentioned that surfing abroad always comes with a learning curve, and you have to always respect the wishes of the locals. Everyone seemed fascinated by the topic, so I relayed a few of my experiences in the water to the group. As usual, there were a few that said they'd always wanted to learn to surf, and asked if I could teach them. I said sure, and that we would find a nice friendly wave to learn on while we were on our trip. Even the two bodyguards were up for it, and said maybe they could trade some self-defense tips for surfing tips. That sounded good to me, I figured these two guys would know exactly what they're doing.

Over the next few days, we traveled around Sydney with Angie, serving as tour guide. She not only knew the city but also the history behind it. I got into my photography role, capturing the sites and the anecdotes of the group. They knew how to have fun, and the different personalities messed together well. Angie invited everyone, including the flight attendants and pilots, so there was a very diverse mix of people; and somehow, we all seemed to get along.

Back at the house, we would split up at times, the ladies would go shopping, and Taylor and I got some training in self-defense. The house had a gym and weight room, so it was a good opportunity to stay in shape and learn from the Jake and Mikhail. They both had backgrounds in martial arts, and after a few lessons I felt like, I could not only defend myself but also counter-attack any oncoming aggression. I've always been one to avoid confrontation, but you never know when you might need to protect yourself or others around you. On the second to the last day, I took a few in the group to a local beach, and we rented some soft surfboards. Most of the group were able to at least stand up by the end of the day, and everyone was laughing at themselves and others when someone fell off. This is what surfing is all about- enjoying yourself and appreciating the ocean and what it does to the human spirit.

On our last day, we packed up and headed to the airport. Next stop- Perth. I'd always wanted to go to Western Australia, and this was my chance. It's the opposite of Sydney, with a rugged coastline, and a somewhat harsh environment. The weather was much cooler, and you had a sense that it was more of a reflection of the old Australia, before the commercialization and impact of colonization. There was still the city life in Perth, but once you left town, it was open territory, and the people in the surrounding areas were much less influenced by modern times and happy to live a simpler life. I was also eager to surf some of their world-famous breaks, having seen contests at Margaret River and the surrounding beaches over the Internet. The plan was to spend a week in the area, then take Angie's yacht, which was harbored in Perth, north to Broome and Southeast Asia. What I was most looking forward to was seeing Estrela. I had been calling her each day, but we both were counting the days until she arrived.

The itinerary included a trip to Swan Valley's vineyards, a trip to Rottnest Island, a tour covering the history of the Aboriginals' life and their ceremonies, and some free time to enjoy the beautiful beaches. The second day was a beach day. I rented a car, and Taylor and I headed for Margaret River. It's one of the iconic surf breaks of Australia. It is a long reef break, breaking left and right, making it ideal for drawn-out turns and a ski-like approach. A modest swell from the Indian Ocean provided us with head high plus waves, but the cold water and offshore winds kept our blood pumping inside our wetsuits. The line-up was spread out, so that made it easier for Taylor to get waves, and freed me to go to the outside and pick off a few set waves. I love this kind of wave, it suits my style and reminds me of snowboarding in Mammoth; taking the gondola to the cornice, and carving the face with long sweeping power carves. Taylor got some good ones off the left takeoff position, and after two hours we were cold but worked. The inside was tricky, with exposed rocks and swirling waters. We talked about how to avoid any difficult encounters with the inside, and we watched how the locals did things, which is always a good idea.

We drove back to the house, and hit the shower. Angie would be meeting with some business clients on the other side of town for dinner, so I took Taylor, Marnie, Jake and Rochelle to a local pub for dinner. We had a few beers, and Taylor even had one. In Australia, you can have beer if you're accompanied by an adult, and are having food. Towards the end of our dinner, a couple of rowdy locals came to our table and asked Marnie and Rochelle if they could buy them a drink. They politely declined, saying we'd be leaving soon. One of the locals yelled out, "Americans, ha, think you're too good for everyone else."

Jake spoke up, "We are not looking for trouble, you should apologize to the ladies".

I knew this could turn ugly, so I said, "We should be going."

As we started to stand up, one of the locals pushed Jake-wrong thing to do. Jake grabbed his arm and twisted it behind his back, and pushed him against the bar. The other guy jumped on Jake's back. I punched the guy in the kidney, which caused him to release Jake and grab his backside. Jake spun the guy against the bar around, and rammed him head first into the other guy. They both went down. Jake stood over them and said, "Enough? Don't get up, we're done here". With that, the group headed for the door as Jake stood over the two downed Aussies. I put enough cash on the bar to cover our tab, plus a healthy tip, saying to the bartender, "Sorry mate, didn't want any trouble."

When we got to the car, I said, "Well, that was fun."

Everyone laughed, but I could tell this was a bit disturbing, and there was a nervous vibe in the air.

"Nice punch, I told you kidney shots from the back work every time," Jake told me.

"I really didn't think I'd actually have to use it. Thanks for taking control."

The rest of the group chimed in with a, "Yes Jake, thank you."

The next morning, we gathered around the dining room table and had coffee. Marnie relayed the story from the night before, and Jake said it was nothing really. When Angie heard I added a little assist to the skirmish, she turned to me and said, "Renee, that's something new for you. How did you do that?"

"Jake and Mikhail showed me a couple of things. To be honest, I haven't been part of a fight since high school, and that was not my doing."

"Pianists have to be careful, we don't want any broken fingers. Are you okay?"

"Yes, of course. I punched a soft spot", which brought out a few laughs.

We visited an Aboriginal village, and our guide was a local man that has worked hard to keep their traditions and rituals intact and uninfluenced by outside cultures. Angie contributes to a fund that allows them to keep large areas of land for themselves, but still allowing occasional visits from health care professionals and environmental agencies to make sure they are protected from fires and other natural disasters. It's easy to see the association between the plight of the American Indians and that of the Aborigines. As our world shrinks smaller and smaller, and technology closes in on our personal freedoms, my hope is that we tread lightly on more primitive cultures that may be discovered over the next few decades.

The next day Estrela would be arriving, and most of the group was taking a beach day, so I drove to the airport with Angie and Mikhail. When she got off the plane and entered the airport, I called out her name and gave a wave in her direction.

"Renee!" she yelled and we ran together, hugged and kissed.

"I missed you, I'm so glad you're here," I said staring at her with teary eyes.

Angie came over and Estrela grabbed her hand and said, "Thank you so much, this means the world to me!" And though it was said in Portuguese, the meaning was clear to Angie.

"We are so glad you could come!" Angie replied, and again though it was said in English, no translation was necessary.

We grabbed her luggage off the carousel, walked to the car, and drove back. It was a beautiful sunny day, so we all changed and joined the rest of the group at the beach. Estrela had been on planes for nearly twenty hours, and a chance to unwind in the warm sun was a perfect way to relax and stretch out. When we returned to the house, Angie ordered dinner to be delivered, and it was a chance to introduce Estrela to the group. Rochelle spoke Portuguese, having spent her childhood in Brazil. She acted as translator, and everyone had questions for Estrela. We all ended up staying up late, drinking wine and telling stories.

The next morning, we all packed and headed down to the marina, where the captain joined us along with two crew members. The yacht was huge, with multiple levels and decks. Angie gave us a guided tour, and showed each of us where our cabins were. After we settled in, Estrela and I went out on the main deck and said goodbye to Perth. The captain had informed us that the weather looked good for the next few days, and the seas should be calm.

Our destination was Broome, and it would take a few days to get there. There were plenty of things to do, and though we did join the others in a variety of activities, Estrela and I spent a good deal of time in our cabin. There was a grand piano in the main dining room, so Estrela and I would sneak in and practice a bunch of songs. I brought a songbook of jazz tunes, and many were of Latin composers with lyrics in Portuguese. I brought in Rochelle for a couple of sessions, and she helped translate a few tunes written in English to Portuguese. Often times musicians prefer to practice in private. It's easier to get things done when there's no audience. Occasionally we would have people walk through while we were rehearsing, but fortunately they seemed to understand that it was practice, not a performance.

The night before arriving in Broome, Angie spelled out some of the activities she had planned, and other options for our free time. She has an investment in the pearl industry there, and she suggested that while she was at a meeting, she had scheduled the rest of us to take a tour of a pearl farm, which included a boat ride to see some of the shells growing in the crystal blue waters. The beaches were beautiful, so everyone wanted to spend some time in the sun. On the third night, Angie had a party planned at her ranch, and Estrela and I would play as a duet for Angie's guests. We also were looking forward to some horseback riding and a camel ride along the beach.

Once we docked, we took a small shuttle to Angie's ranch a few miles inland. She gave us a quick tour and showed us to our rooms. Estrela wanted to shower before dinner, and Jake said he wanted to do a quick workout and asked if I wanted to join him. He showed me some ways to defend myself in case I was ever attacked, and he gave me a ten-inch club made of ironwood. He demonstrated how it could be used to block a punch, and how a sharp blow to the wrist would cripple an assailant, and that this would also protect my hands from injury. Although I didn't think I needed it, when you're in a foreign country and you're unfamiliar with the area, foreigners are often targets for thieves and kidnappers. He also gave me a small holster that would attach to my belt and would make it easy to grab on the spot.

Over the next few days, we visited the pearl farm, did some riding, and took some dune buggies out behind the ranch for some off-road fun. The night of the party, we met some of Angie's business partners, many coming from Southeast Asia that had flown in for her meeting. Estrela wore a full-length black dress, with shoulder straps and a slit along the left side. I wore the tux I had gotten back in LA, with a black dress shirt and a black tie. After dinner, Estrela and I played a few songs for everyone, then Angie suggested that anyone who wanted to could go for a swim in the pool, which was a perfect way to cool off in the warm humid air. Estrela was a little reluctant to change out of her dress, but I talked her into it after a couple drinks from the bar. The heated pool, star-studded sky, and balmy air provided a perfect combination of the elements for a night swim. A few of our group joined us, along with a couple of the younger guests and Angie. This was really fun, and everyone was laughing and splashing around like a bunch of kids. When we got out of the pool, Angie had some long comfortable robes for everyone, for those that didn't want to change back into their party clothes. There was a more casual vibe after this, and Angie played some dance music over her house music system. Even the older guests eventually got out on the dance floor. This was how Angie was; she could be at one moment very formal and traditional, and the next moment as free as a teenager at their first party. Everyone around her accepted her gregarious personality, and you couldn't help but love the way she made everyone feel welcome and appreciated. Estrela and I felt like one of the family, and we became even closer knowing we were unconditionally accepted for who we were. After the party, we thanked Angie for such a fun evening, and thanked her again for inviting us on the trip.

The next day everyone slept in a bit, then had breakfast and drove down to the beach. Angie had to meet with some clients at the pearl farm that afternoon, so a few of us decided to have dinner at a local brewery. The Aussies love their beer, and the atmosphere was loud and chaotic. Jake had suggested I bring my Billy club, just in case things got too rowdy since Mikhail was with Angie, and he wanted everyone to be safe. I hovered over Estrela, making sure she was comfortable and at ease. There were some attractive women in our group, and the Aussies are not shy about approaching any woman, whether they're with men or not. The ladies in our group politely declined the advances of a few, but we could tell it was about time to go after about an hour. As we were leaving, a couple of locals stood up and stepped in front of us. The bartender yelled out, "Hey, step aside, these are nice folks and I don't want any trouble in here." I had my hand on the club, but fortunately the two locals stepped aside and let us pass. Jake is a very intimidating figure, so he always leads us when we're in a sketchy place. Everything worked out fine, and we headed back to the ranch.

In the morning, we gathered around the dining area, and Angie said she had a surprise destination for us if we were interested. "How does everyone feel about going to Bangkok for a couple days?" I was all in, I've always wanted to go there, and this was an easy yes for me. The whole group let out a resounding yes, with a number of people chiming in with responses similar to my thoughts. "Great! It will take a few days to get there, but I think you'll love it. The Thai people are really friendly, and the cultural experience is second to none. It can be a little dangerous in some places, so we will have to stay together and not wander into any place that could lead us into trouble." Rochelle translated for

Estrela, but I could tell she was very excited, and she reached over and put her arms around my neck and was kind of bouncing up and down with joy.

We arrived at the Chao Phraya River delta, and cruised up the river into Bangkok. Angie had business associates in Bangkok, and one of them had set up a beautiful house for us to stay in. We settled in and had dinner prepared by a local chef that came to the house. We all had a few drinks, then went to bed early. The next morning Angie had a business meeting in the city, so Mikhail accompanied her, and the rest of us went shopping in an open-air market, with a local guide that had worked for Angie on previous trips. It was a fairly safe area, geared for tourists, with an amazing assortment of local art, fashion, and foods that filled the air with exotic smells. There were so many sights and sounds that Jake had his hands full trying to keep everyone together and out of reach of pickpockets and scammers. I kept Estrela close, but her curiosity was hard to contain. At around 1:00 pm, our guide led us to a restaurant that was surrounded by gardens and ponds, and a maze we were guided through by the maître de. After lunch we visited a Buddhist temple, and an old Hindu sanctuary. Thailand has had hundreds of years of influence by both religions, and a history of political unrest. Our guide was well versed in Thailand's history, and though his English was a little hard to understand, we all got a quick education.

We got a call from Angie, who wanted us to meet her at another famous restaurant for dinner. It was in the red-light district, and was known for its crazy nightlife, an abundance of prostitutes, and being a place where a person can find just about anything they want. At about 7:00, we met up with Angie and Mikhail. She had made a reservation earlier, so we were seated at a table on the second floor overlooking the crazy street life. There was a mix of tourists, scammers, hookers, drug dealers, and street entertainers. Dinner was amazing, though most of the menu was a blur, because of not speaking Thai and having several rounds of drinks. After dinner, we went down the street to a well-known nightclub. We were about to enter when a man stepped in front of Mikhail and shot him in the chest. Jake stepped in and took a shot in the leg. It didn't slow him down too much as he kicked the shooter's gun from his hand, then punched him in the throat. Another guy grabbed Angie by the arm and attempted to pull her into an alley to a waiting car. I grabbed my club and came down hard on his wrist. I could hear his bone crack, but he came towards me as if he wasn't done. I clubbed him in the head, and he went down. Jake rushed over and took Angie by the arm, and yelled out, "Everyone back to the restaurant. Renee, take Angie and the others; I'm going to see to Mikhail!"

I escorted Angie, Estrela, and the others at a quick pace through the crowd, as police sirens screamed through the air. When we reached the restaurant, we huddled inside the lobby. Two bouncers came over, and Angie seemed to know them. "Go check on Mikhail and Jake, we'll be okay here," she told me.

I flew out the door and headed back to the scene. By now, the police had pushed everyone back, and an ambulance had parked at an angle in the street, blocking vehicle access. I approached an officer closest to me, and told him I was involved in the incident. He looked at me with a sort of confused look, then called over another officer. I repeated my statement to the second officer, and he apparently understood enough English to make out what I was saying. He took me by the arm and walked me over to his superior. I looked over towards the ambulance and saw Mikhail be loaded in on a gurney, and Jake in a wheelchair being wrapped around the leg. I broke off from my escort and quickly walked over to the ambulance. Jake said, "I'm okay, it went in and out and missed the main artery. The medic thinks Mikhail will make it through, looks like it missed his lungs, and he'll probably have a broken rib or two". "How's everyone else doing?" he asked.

"They're good, just shaken up. I wish I could have done more."

"You did good. Thanks for stepping in."

"Sure," I replied. The officer in charge spoke English, so I relayed the details of the shooting to him. Another paramedic was attending to the guy Jake hit. A second ambulance had pulled up, and they placed the guy I clubbed on a gurney and rolled him to the open back door. The three of us gave our IDs and passports to the lead officer, and a contact phone number. There were witnesses being interviewed, and they must have confirmed our statements, because I was told I was free to go. I got the name of the hospital Jake and Mikhail would be taken to, and then hurried back to the group. Once I got there, I told them, "They're going to be okay, I think. It looks like Mikhail got the worst of it, but should recover fine. The bullet that hit Jake passed through his leg and missed his main artery. I got the info on the hospital they'll be taken to; we should go back to the house."

"Yes, definitely. Renee, could you get the car and pull it out front? Text me when you get here." Angie said.

"Of course, be right back."

The restaurant manager said I should drive around to the alley behind the restaurant to avoid the crowds in the street. I kissed Estrela and headed back to the car. I pulled up in the back of the restaurant, and gave Angie a text. The group came out the back door, escorted by the manager. Everyone climbed in, and we drove back to the house. There was an eerie silence in the car, and people were huddled together, consoling each other. We arrived at the house, and Angie had everyone come to the living room. "I'm so sorry. I don't know who these people were, but hopefully the police will find out. I'm going to call the hospital now. Let's just pray for Jake and Mikhail". "Renee, thank you so much for what you did. I don't know what would have happened if you had not been there". I nodded in response. My arm was around Estrela, who was still very upset and trying to hold back her tears. We all retired to our rooms, and Angie consoled the ladies and walked them to their rooms.

In the morning, we gathered around the dining room table, and we could see Angie in the kitchen talking to the hospital. After a few minutes, she joined the group. "They're both doing good. Jake will be released later today, and Mikhail came out of surgery in good shape. I want to apologize again, this has never happened before, and I'm so thankful our two guys are doing well".

There was a few thank gods around the room, and there was a little sense of relief on everyone's face. The day plans were put on hold, and Angie had a chef come in for the day. The sun was out, and the sky was a clear blue. The group spent the day out on the deck in the backyard. Estrela was feeling much better, and we even managed a laugh or two. Around 4:00, Jake arrived. We all greeted him, and with the help of a crutch, he walked inside. He turned to me and said, "Thanks, buddy. You did the right thing."

"No problem. We're all just so thankful for you and Mikhail."

We were scheduled to fly back to LA in two days, so we took in as many sites as we could. The day after the incident, we all went down to the hospital where Mikhail was being cared for. He seemed in good spirits, and the doctor told us he was a very strong patient, and he should heal up quickly. Jake decided to stick around an extra couple of days so he could fly home with Mikhail. On the day of our flight, Angie told us that the pilots that had been staying in Perth had flown to Bangkok, and the jet was fueled and prepped for our flight back, with a stopover in Honolulu. This would be a long flight home, but everyone was anxious to return to their own beds, and see the people they had missed. For Estrela and I, it would be a long and beautiful relationship, for which I will forever be grateful.

Made in the USA
Columbia, SC
25 September 2022

67810527R00086